Tales of Wonder
The Saga of Stickitville

A Comedy

First and Maybe Final Draft

by

Richard R. Wyly, Sr.

Tales of Wonder: The Saga of Stickitville
Copyright © 2019 by Richard R. Wyly

Tellwell Talent
www.tellwell.ca

ISBN
978-0-2288-1701-7 (Hardcover)
978-0-2288-1700-0 (Paperback)
978-0-2288-1702-4 (eBook)

Reviews

Tales of Wonder
The Saga of Stickitville

"Richard Wyly has a unique writing style, and his quirky characters were fun to follow."

— Karen Sorensen

"The book is delightfully clever and very original in its approach. An extra-funny read for anyone who has ever worked in the clothing industry. The chapter on the history of underwear is a blast — it's pure wacko."

— Jim Lillard, retired entrepreneur
and Master of Creative Living

"The writer gives us a lighthearted read with lots of good imagination. .... The gerbil burgers sound delicious! Love the attention to detail, and the way the author pokes fun at some of the major icons in the traditional clothing business. Absolutely hilarious."

— William J. Cardoza, apparel executive
President/Owner, Red Moon Enterprises Ltd.

"Unrenowned author Richard Wyly, Sr., has put together a Saga book, under his umbrella *Tales of Wonder*, filled with a multitude of peppery characters. It is a little comic mountain drama about a Rowdy Rodeo Days Extravaganza and so many other happenings that will have readers laughing from beginning to end."

— Terry Wilmot, Ph.D.
Retired psychologist and educator

In loving memory of our son
Richard R. Wyly, Jr.
1960–2016

Table of Contents

Introduction

Getting a sense of who, what and where is really important in setting up this very significant literary experience, which I am submitting to all of you enlightened readers. Pay attention, folks; otherwise you might get lazy and think that you have got it all figured out. Fat chance! Get ready for the reading ride of your life, or not. It's a comedy, and I hope it makes you laugh yourself silly.

This ongoing "saga" is set in a beautiful mountain village high in the Rockies, somewhat west of a delightful little hamlet known to many as Old Laffinatcha Meadows. Our small town has a name: we call it Stickitville. Our founding fathers, and probably a few of the mothers, found themselves seriously "stuck" in Stickitville. It happened right after the great flood of 1872. The chosen leader of these misguided but brave souls was none other than Colonel JJ Eberhart. We have a statue of him in the town square, which the pigeons decorate regularly. There will be more on him later.

Most of the time our little mountain berg is orderly, progressive and loyal to the North American way of life. Sometimes it gets a bit crazy, especially during holidays and of course at Stickitville's two major annual events: the Yucca Days Festival and, two weeks later, the Rowdy Rodeo Days Extravaganza. Each of these events features a community parade, a music festival and a Barbecue Cook-Off Contest, featuring chicken and ribs for the Yucca Days Festival, and custom designer cheeseburgers for the Rowdy Rodeo Days Extravaganza. People come from far and wide just to party and watch the strange behaviors that some of our citizens express during these celebrations. Each festival lasts for four days. Our Hero Billy, the community leader, says, "Thank heaven for that."

The out-of-town visitors have also noticed that there seems to be a large number of fully grown yucca plants all over the landscape; they are on the mountainsides, up and down the rivers and all over the lower valley. The flower, or the plume, that sits on top of the yucca plants seems ready to explode as they mature during the summer season. When one gets close to the cluster of bulbs on the tall plant, it becomes possible to feel the vibration and the magnetic pulse coming from the bright yellow-orange plume. For some folks, it almost has a hypnotic power.

A few of the iconic landmarks and places you will want to discover would be where our locals hang out, along with what transpires within. Also, you will want to know about some of our citizens who are the standout characters to be portrayed in this sometimes outrageous story — thus the name *Tales of Wonder: The Saga of Stickitville*.

One of the primary social hubs is Squeaky's Pool Hall. It is a classic billiards joint with several tables that have seen better days. They show the wear and tear of too many schooners of spilled beer and cigars that have been ground out on the pool table railings and on the dark green felt tops.

The pool hall has a back lounge that is for members only. "The Back Room Meeting Place" is what the locals call it. It has old worn-out leather couches, heavy wooden chairs and tables, a few bar stools and a fireplace that doesn't work very well. It would be pushing it to refer to it as a well-thought-out clubhouse.

The Boogie Woogie Burger Bar is the main joint for burgers, beer and tacos. No pizzas — nope, not a single combo or pepperoni-mushroom in sight. The decor is simple but elegant, the place comfortable and clean. It would be best described as cozy.

The main players in this adventure are as follows:

1. William Cardoza, legendary leader and mentor, known as Our Hero Billy
2. The Cardoza Playboys, Stickitville's esteemed fraternal order, loyal to Our Hero Billy. Membership is by invitation only.
3. Jim Carl Lillard, owner of Squeaky's Pool Hall and the Back Room Meeting Place
4. Joe Bob Pickens, our "nearly blind" philosopher
5. Stinky, our hippie and the local part-time deputy
6. Charlie Mack Pearlman, owner of Pearlman's Towing and six-time Barbecue Cook-Off Contest champion
7. Natasha, owner of Natasha's Salvage Yard. Shares same last name with Cher.
8. Darla May McIntire, fancy line dance instructor

9. Carla Jo McIntire, co-owner of Blaster's Beauty Shop, and Darla May's identical twin sister

10. Arthur Ray Rahn, a.k.a. Luke the Drifter; Curator of the Roby E. Smith Memorial Institute

11. Amy Jean Ruggles, manager of Squeaky's Pool Hall and the Back Room Meeting Place

12. Eddie Wayne Geisler, our "Steely-Eyed" Sheriff of Stickitville

13. Officer "Slats" O'Reilly, the tall, skinny cop

14. Officer "Snapper" McCoy, the short, pudgy cop

15. "Spunky" Dan Carlson, Mayor of Stickitville

16. Maggie Anne Proctor, owner of the Boogie Woogie Burger Bar

17. Dr. Mikey Lamar Cook, physician, lawyer and Girl Scout troop leader

18. Sonny Barbados, world champ rodeo bronc rider

19. Elva June Ridley, women's world champ rodeo barrel racer

20. Consuelo Rodriguez, wealthy Mexican beauty and horticulturist

21. Maynard, a mysterious visionary and itinerant man of knowledge

Prologue

So, the story begins as Our Hero Billy was traveling in the massive Rocky Mountain wilderness along a dusty dirt road late in the afternoon in his restored all-black 1967 MGB roadster with chrome wire wheels and refitted with a Lotus twin-cam 200 h.p. engine. (Maynard says it's a car-guy thing.) On Billy's left was the Gray Lakes Campground, located on the 18-mile stretch of deep water that feeds the Crow River basin. For the last two hours there had been zero traffic in either direction.

Suddenly, he noticed in his mirror an old beater minivan speeding up behind him, looking to pass. As this bozo blasted by, he showered the MGB with loads of gravel, rocks and dust. Enough to choke a giraffe sitting on the top of a skyscraper. Our Hero Billy sped up to confront this jerk and at least give him the "flying finger of fate." Billy was also aware that the road ahead was about to change into steep drop-offs and sharp curves.

Around the second curve, there was a huge thrust of dirt exploding into the air. The minivan had crashed, rolling over several times and landing against a large pine tree at about a 45-degree angle.

Billy set aside his anger for the moment and decided to climb down from the road's edge and see if he could help this wretched idiot. He made his way into the ravine to determine whether or not the fool was still alive. The reckless jerk was bent over and still strapped in behind the steering wheel. Barely breathing was a red-headed, long-haired, stinky hippie who was knocked out like a light.

He looked around inside the van and noticed some strange-looking packages wrapped in brown butcher paper. One of them was torn open and some fine white powder had spilled out on the minivan's floor.

Aha! Aha! Our Hero Billy had got himself a real-live drug dealer here, and there was still not a wiggle from this wretched schmuck. He was clearly out cold.

Billy was crawling further back into the van to check it all out, when he noticed at least five old, full-size matching leather suitcases. He opened the nearest one to him and nearly fainted at what was inside.

Yep, you guessed it. Smiling up at Billy were stacks of professionally and beautifully wrapped bundles of "cold hard American cash." There were packs of twenties, fifties and hundred-dollar bills. A close estimate under the pressure of the moment indicated that he was looking at perhaps eight or nine hundred thousand freshly printed Yankee bucks. Maybe even more than a million smackers, all Billy's just for the taking.

Hey, let's wait a minute here; Our Hero is no common opportunist. What low-life would do such a thing? Certainly not our Billy. What to do, oh whatever should he do? Hmmm.

As he was wrestling with all of this, the scumbag hippy-dippy drug dealer groaned and moaned, and burped just for good measure. Billy rolled "Stinky" over on his back and, as if there hadn't already been enough excitement for the day, discovered that the man was wearing a Coyote Sportswear coveted first-edition all-cotton tee-shirt. It was the white one, complete with longer tail and double topstitching. The bright yellow-orange plume stood proudly atop the yucca plant embroidery. Simply put, it was the most valuable of all the collector shirts from anyone, including those from "old polo pony Ralph." You know, what's-his-name: Lif-chitz or something like that. (Maynard says he knows him personally.)

To be sure, owning and wearing Coyote Sportswear is a pathway to truth and therefore justice, as well as being a sign of darn good taste. Along, of course, with a good supply of yucca dust.

Now Our Hero Billy was really faced with a monumental decision. Would it be the drugs, the cash or the icon of all tee-shirts? Oh, what would he do?

The next morning, Our Hero heard a knock on his door; two mean-looking police officers were standing in front of him with a serious demeanor and a frown. They had been practising the "mantra of cop snarling" just before leaving the patrol car. Apparently, it's in the cop manual and you are supposed to do it if making an arrest is imminent.

The taller of the two cops, Officer Slats O'Reilly, said to Billy that someone had seen his "little black sporty car" up on the Gray Lakes Road, near where a minivan had rolled off into the ravine yesterday. The pudgy, shorter cop, Officer Snapper McCoy, then asked Billy if he knew anything about the accident or if he had seen this hippie character who was walking down the road, in somewhat of a stupor and shirtless. Officer McCoy went on to mention, "The hippie was muttering something about matching leather suitcases and brown butcher paper–wrapped packages."

It's important to note right here that by this time Charlie Mack Pearlman of Pearlman Towing Co. had already towed Stinky's van to Natasha's Salvage Yard. "Steely-Eyed" Sheriff Eddie Wayne Geisler then had the van impounded and hidden out of sight in the salvage yard. Sniffer dogs were brought in but found nothing. The dogs did smile a lot, though. We think they were on to something, as there was lots of tell-tale tail wagging.

Our Hero Billy shrugged his shoulders and said, "Must have been someone else, Officer. Sorry, I'd truly like to help out. I hope the hippie lad is okay."

With that, the cops thanked him for his time. As they were leaving, Officer Slats, the taller cop, looked back over his shoulder and said to Billy, "Nice tee-shirt ya got there, Sport. Is that a Coyote tee-shirt? I really like the floral design atop the yucca. Hee hee hee. Maybe I'll get one for myself."

We've always known that Our Hero would do the right thing. Will he? Hmmm... Stay tuned.

Part One

Yucca Days Festival

Chapter One

Stickitville Antics

Fast-forward a few months. Squeaky's Pool Hall was now owned by none other than Jim Carl Lillard. He took over the business from Arthur Ray Rahn, also known as "Luke the Drifter." Luke had moved on to manage the Roby E. Smith Memorial Institute here in Stickitville. This was a place near the library where lost or seriously damaged souls could get a free lunch, along with an army surplus cot to sleep on for a couple of days. After that the army pit bull cop dogs chased the no-good bums out of town. The pit bulls had a good time, and the bums were okay because the army cots were stiff and the lunch wasn't worth a darn, anyway. Cold tuna fish and no-salt crackers. Yuck.

The Cardoza Playboys weren't happy that Jim Carl was taking over Squeaky's Pool Hall. First thing he did was raise the ball-racking fee from $1.00 to $3.00. The Playboys held several meetings about this two-dollar gouge he'd imposed on them. They wondered if they should boycott the pool hall.

Cooler heads prevailed and they decided not to boycott. They would lose the right to use the Back Room Meeting Place. The truth is they would also lose contact with Amy Jean Ruggles. None of Billy's Playboys wanted that; you see, Amy Jean was the barmaid and manager for the Back Room Meeting Place. By the way, our lovely barmaid was a world-class, eye-popping beauty.

Amy Jean wanted the Playboys to stay around. The tips were great and she always made it worth their while, occasionally tossing in kisses and a hug or two. The truth is she didn't want to risk her special friendship with Joe Bob Pickens. He being nearly blind, she allowed him a gentle caress and a smooch on her lovely cheek — all out of sympathy, as he couldn't see very well, or that's what we thought. Amy Jean didn't really mind, because Joe Bob let her play with his renowned bushy red hair and wide, muscular shoulders. She also enjoyed how his abs rippled all the way down to his five-pocket denim jeans styled by the Coyote Sportswear design team.

Eventually, everyone was happy to continue supporting Squeaky's Pool Hall. The Cardoza Playboys all agreed to keep secret the relationship between Amy Jean and Joe Bob.

Late Friday nights, the Playboys always drew straws to see who would get to watch Joe Bob and Amy Jean makin' out through a neatly crafted peephole high above them, between the rafters in the floor of the attic above the Back Room Meeting Place. The couch in the meeting room was in the right place for viewing. Joe Bob would show off his artful hugging and squeezing away at the behest of a delighted and sometimes squeaking Amy Jean. She loved learning, or trying to learn, Joe Bob's techniques and his unusual, creative movements. She had good balance. For that we give her much credit and high marks. Her pool hall scores improved dramatically.

Joe Bob had developed a technical workout position he called the "double reverse over-and-under librarian's toehold squeeze." This all went as planned every Friday night, until Natasha and Darla May McIntire heard about it. Both felt that

Joe Bob was a two-timing, no-good SOB, and they were gonna get him for this transgression.

So Friday night rolled around again, just as it did every Friday night, only this night would go down in history. It would forever be highlighted and known as the recognized tale when one speaks about our famous pool hall and the special Back Room Meeting Place.

Natasha and Darla May decided that they would crash the party. "Crash" is a key word here, as you will soon see. Upon arriving, Darla May pulled out her 356 Magnum and ordered the Cardoza Playboys to drop their beers, raise their arms and remain silent. She then got herself busy tugging and teasing and tickling the Playboys to see if any of them could giggle like Joe Bob. And when asked why, she said, "Well, you never know when he might just up and die on us. What then? Who ya gonna call?"

None could match the finesse of Joe Bob and his magical "lucky-ducky power dance moves." The performance was certainly of Smithsonian quality in a historical sense. We have it on good authority that pictures have been requested.

Natasha climbed up into the rafters to watch and to catch Joe Bob and Amy doing the couch smooch. It's important to remember the rage and disdain that Natasha and Darla May held against Joe Bob and Amy Jean for cheating on them.

Well, the usual act started and was proceeding with the regular kissing and hugging, pinching, joking and stroking, when all of a sudden the rafters gave way to Natasha's 250-plus pounds. It was an awkward 14-foot sort of swan-dive drop, smack through the coffee table in front of the couch and onto the floor. Security cameras caught the whole thing in slo-mo. The crash to the floor could be heard clear across the valley, causing widespread panic among the citizens here in Stickitville. Jim Carl nearly had a heart attack, and for weeks, cows wouldn't give milk, chickens wouldn't lay eggs, and frightened children were escorted to school by their nervous, paranoid parents.

Joe Bob didn't see a thing; he's nearly blind, you know. The Cardoza Playboys agreed to play dumb and ride it out, hoping for the best. Amy Jean moved to the next town with her awesome blue eyes and knuckle-deep dimples. She quickly got another job, as a "girl spot welder" at the tractor factory.

Spunky Dan Carlson, Mayor of Stickitville, was besieged by citizens demanding that something be done about the nonsense before the annual Barbecue Cook-Off Contest. So it was Our Hero Billy Cardoza to the rescue. Billy decided to load up on yucca dust to get to the truth of the matter and therefore find justice. It's his job in life, of course. Billy told "Steely-Eyed" Sheriff Eddie Wayne Geisler to let Stinky out of jail (remember Stinky?), as he thought he would make a good deputy and get to the bottom of this social unrest, once and for all.

Natasha was still in the hospital with multiple broken bones and cuts and bruises. Billy had Darla May turn in her 356 Magnum and thanked her for having the good sense to not shoot anyone. He told Joe Bob to lie low and keep his buff, bushy, red-headed self out of sight.

Charlie Mack Pearlman showed his loyalty to Natasha, staying by her side as she recovered. He was concerned that she might not be well enough to host the annual Fourth of July Barbecue Cook-Off Contest at the salvage yard. Charlie Mack was looking for a seventh win, even though the suspicion of his cheating lingered on. (Maynard wants to know exactly how one cheats at barbecuing.)

"Steely-Eyed" Sheriff Geisler had taken a liking to Darla May and sent her a five-pound box of Whitman's Sampler Chocolates. She gave most of them to Natasha, who wolfed them right down, then licked her fat, stubby fingers for a while, just because it felt good.

Sheriff Eddie Wayne invited Darla May to join him on his speedboat for the weekend. His boat was one of those old Chris Craft wooden speedsters, model 57, powered by a Ford flathead engine. It leaked too much water to be safe; however, he had a nice foam pad that he intended to stretch out on the floor of the boat in order to play a game of star-search the heavens. This was all for Darla May, as a way of showing off his charm and grace. He was going to teach her what that big sky was all about. She said she would like to do that very much and thanked him for the invitation.

Darla May had never made out on a boat before and probably not in a lot of other places. Oh well, her friends thought she would like it. After all, it was her idea. Uh-huh.

After the star search on the boat, Darla talked facts and wanted to know about our toe-tapping Sheriff dude, who said he was a world-class dancer. She needed to check this out. Some folks said he had won the prestigious South American Dancers Gold Medal two times. He said that the trick is all in the fingers and the hips, especially if you have double-jointed knuckles and a snappy, swiveling ankle movement. He claimed it was more fun than a handful of warm pecans and jelly beans.

"Steely-Eyed" Sheriff Geisler had completely forgotten that there were a bunch of bums in the Stickitville jail. These losers had received no food or water all weekend. Fortunately, someone smuggled in a few hits of yucca dust. It helped, and anyway none of them knew what day it was and they couldn't care less.

Our Hero Billy was really angry at this neglect, so he let the bums out of jail, as long as they promised to behave for the Yucca Days Festival. Being a nice guy, he also got them a free lunch and two beers over at the Boogie Woogie Burger Bar.

Stinky was deputized and given a six-shooter, a badge and a goofy-looking cowboy hat. For some reason, somebody just hadn't ducked quickly enough to dodge the bullet and a hole was put through the top of it. That little incident happened sometime in its life of service. Stinky's duties were to watch over everything and be in charge of crowd control. Facts are, he spent every minute looking for packages wrapped in brown butcher paper and for five full-size matching leather suitcases.

As mentioned earlier, Stinky's minivan had been towed and hidden over at Natasha's Salvage Yard by Pearlman Towing Co. No one so far had said anything about the missing booty. No one had asked Billy Cardoza, except officers Slats O'Reilly and Snapper McCoy.

Very few people knew that officers Slats and Snapper were possibly the role models for the two main characters in the movie *Dumb and Dumber*. In fact, much of the movie was filmed in Stickitville, or so said Our Hero Billy. What could possibly be funnier than that? Also, if you ever saw the TV comedy series "Car 54, Where Are You?" then you, the reader, can get an idea of how these two cops would and did routinely screw up anything and everything they attempted to do on their own. However, things and events would always seem to turn around and bail them out, making them look like heroes. Their luck was incredible. They consistently managed to get their man or woman. Sometimes they actually caught real crooks. This surprising similarity is exactly why Billy saw to it that Slats and Snapper were kept on the payroll. They were also hilarious just to look at — a total copy of the "Mutt and Jeff" cartoon characters, for sure.

* * *

Now back to our unsolved mystery concerning the van crash on the Gray Lakes mountain road. Stinky thought Our Hero Billy knew more than he was telling, as he had been the last person to see the packages wrapped in brown butcher paper, and the five matching full-size leather suitcases. Or had he? How about Charlie Mack Pearlman and Natasha? What about "Steely-Eyed" Sheriff Eddie Wayne Geisler? And how about Joe Bob Pickens? Everyone needed to be held as a material witness and suspect until we got to the bottom of this perplexing "kaffuffel." Our Hero certainly had some explaining to do, as did Charlie Mack and Natasha. (No one asked about Maynard.)

Soon, lots of people were putting their money on old "Steely-Eyed" Sheriff Geisler. You see, he went on to make the down payment on a new boat right after the Chris Craft Model 57 sunk at the dock while he and a delighted Darla May were star gazing atop the foam pad on the floor of the boat. We all knew he didn't have that kind of cash to plunk down for a fancy boat. However, to his credit, the new boat would have a much better removable foam pad on the floor behind the seats. That's, of course, should Darla May decide to go there again. She nearly drowned, by golly, when the boat sank.

Curious was the idea that Joe Bob could be a suspect, as he's nearly blind, you know — or that's what some say.

* * *

Anyway, late in the afternoon, as usual, Joe Bob went off to the gym and the showers to get his daily social-admiration fix. The line in the gym was especially long that day, as several more women were present. Most of them were from out of town and had heard about Joe Bob's colossal and athletic body. It cost a lot of money just to get a glimpse of his famous shower power dance.

There was this one large woman with full-body tattoos and numerous body piercings. Long, greasy, wavy black hair and a giant nose ring. Somebody said she offered Joe Bob $10,000 if he would let her tattoo a picture of herself somewhere on his fit and perfect physique. He declined, saying he wouldn't be able to enjoy the art of it all, because he's nearly blind, you know. He did see the humor in it, but thankfully his integrity prevailed.

Billy was really ticked off at Stinky for suggesting that somehow he, our highly respected community guide and mentor, could be involved in something illegal. Billy also wanted to know how someone like Stinky, a common bum, could have ended up with an iconic Coyote Sportswear all-cotton tee-shirt, topstitched, classic in design, with longer tail and the yucca plant embroidery. And of course, always held in high esteem was the magic plume in the traditional bright yellow-orange color.

In the case of the real yucca plant, the bulbs of the plume were packed with the magical and coveted yucca dust. If you looked closely, you would see and feel the pulsing, the anticipation and the explosion. Thus the release of the gift. It happened in the "eye blink" of a nano-second. A huge shower of silver star-like sparkles danced around and covered the sky. Off in the distance, soft crackling and rumbling thunder with bold streaks of lightning filled in with the background sounds. Angels sat on puffy clouds, strumming and plucking their magic harps. Joe Bob was strumming and plucking his magic twanger. Yep, the mayor, Spunky Dan Carlson, sold tickets for that performance also. What a greedy, self-centered jerk.

As one inhaled the sky and the sparkles from the yucca dust, one could complete the promise of a journey down the path to enlightenment, where all would find truth and therefore justice. Or not. Some just got flat-out stoned, enjoying the extended fuzzy sensations, visual ecstasy and some real fine mountain blessings.

Jim Carl Lillard called a meeting of the Cardoza Playboys to see if they could help out poor old bashed-up Natasha. He had already billed her for the coffee table and the rafter repair. He would not press charges, as he didn't know about the peephole. (Neither did Maynard.)

Privately, once Jim Carl found out about it, he was ticked off 'cause he hadn't had a chance to "peep" for himself. Soon everybody in town knew about it, and they were all ticked off as well 'cause they hadn't had a chance to "peep," either. It was reported that some guy named Tom actually did peep.

Jim Carl decided to raise the rent for the Back Room Meeting Place by 67 bucks a month. None of the Cardoza Playboys complained, you see, because Sheriff Geisler had already figured out how to have a better peephole by using lasers and mirrors. The best benefit was that one would no longer have to climb up into the rafters and risk crashing to the floor as Natasha had done. Another benefit was that now, with the magic of video, they were going to have replays and slow motion when it made sense to artfully edit and adjust the sounds. Fantastic, especially since the Back Room Meeting Place was going to charge outsiders to watch. The Cardoza Playboys wouldn't have to sweat the rent increase. "Everybody wins."

After the meeting in the Back Room Meeting Place, they all went down to the Boogie Woogie Burger Bar to get two beers and some burgers and to practise the latest jitterbug dance moves. Maggie Anne Proctor and Dr. Mikey Lamar Cook were really good at it.

Being the owner of the bar, Maggie Anne was suspicious about all this enthusiasm. She decided to hire Stinky to investigate; after all, he was the only appointed deputy serving as a detective, or should that be a defective detective. He did have a badge, a six-shooter, and a cowboy hat with a gunshot hole through the top of it. Seems qualified to me.

Jim Carl was going to have to wait to get a date with Darla May. You see, with Natasha out of commission, Darla May had Joe Bob all to herself.

She had heard of his masterful methods of super-sport hugging and cuddling. She was impressed, and eager to try 'em all out. Not only was Joe Bob a genius at the "double reverse over-and-under librarian's toehold squeeze," he had perfected the "super-sport cluster hug." It was the "one-foot-off-the-couch, firecracker floor-stompin' threesome slide." "THREESOME?" — Darla May frowned and at the same time wondered, would the third party to this event be another woman, or another man?

At this point Joe Bob wanted to keep his options open. Just in case the threesome idea got some traction, he always kept the king-size all-silk bedsheets ready and a fresh quart jar of mayonnaise handy for sandwiches. The mayo was way better than Wesson oil — or olive oil, which he had learned from his old squeeze Miss Crow Valley Pattie. She said it doesn't leave you with that oily taste. (Maynard says, "Mayonnaise? Olive oil? Really?")

In the meantime, Darla May indulged herself by playfully smooching with Joe Bob and enjoying his sweet manly movements in any and every place she could think of. Sometimes twice a day. She considered it a form of aerobic exercise. More than once, at the end of the day, she was heard to murmur the words "Boy howdy, this guy is really something — *Boom-a-Laka, Boom-a-Laka, Sis-Boom-Bah.*"

Meanwhile, Amy Jean Ruggles was spot welding her way into the record books at the tractor factory over in the little town known as Old Laffinatcha Meadows, which has a rich history that all started with Colonel JJ Eberhart and King Letzal B. Laffinatcha.

Letzal was a Viking ruler who in 1872 hitched a ride in a hot-air balloon from the shores of Finland to the Crow Valley, near what is today referred to as Stickitville. Our Viking king had heard of the terrible flood and just wanted to help out. He survived the balloon trip by eating hundreds of bratwurst-and-sour-pickle sandwiches. He also drank hundreds of cases of Reindeer beer.

Documents tell us that King Letzal B. Laffinatcha crash-landed in a terrible storm on a dark and dreary night in the Crow Valley. Citizens rushed over to save him. Right away everyone noticed that Letzal's breath was the absolute worst anyone could remember or even imagine. It had to be the bratwurst-and-sour-pickle sandwiches. The foul air caused mayhem in the valley: Local birds flew south a month early, and even the ones that couldn't fly took off as well. Worms dug deeper into the soil in a massive, wiggling frenzy. Leaves turned brown way before they were supposed to, snakes could neither hiss nor rattle. Dogs and cats huddled together for self-preservation. The mighty gerbils, however, stood their ground. Their breath was even worse, so to get between the two of them the local citizens decided to build an atmospheric barrier that was designed and finished in record time. The valley was saved. Hmmm!!

The rescue committee stored King Letzal's beat-up hot-air balloon in a cave somewhere and saved it for a return trip. Eventually, Colonel JJ and Letzal struck up a real fine "good buddy" friendship — playing checkers, pinching rocks and spinning wooden tops in the dirt. It is said that the two of them wrote the rules for playing modern Shark Games, a challenging and mysterious pastime still going on today. These days, most folks just call it hide-and-seek.

Our nearly blind philosopher, Joe Bob Pickens, would often tell stories in the Back Room Meeting Place about King Letzal B. Laffinatcha, as it had been discovered that Joe Bob was a direct descendent of the Viking king. His bright red bushy hair was the tipoff, for sure. The tales he would tell could enlighten and mesmerize the many boggled minds of those listening. Too much beer and yucca dust did the rest.

One of his most famous — always requested — "brain-stretching tales" was about how King Letzal convinced the young local ladies he would eventually be friends with to learn the art of yodeling. Those who were good at it held a special place of honor among his many relationships. It was apparently a particular and highly intense turn-on for him to hear the yodeling while they were dancing at the up-sided Diddley Doo-Dah Barn Dance Soirée. "O Lee Op Tee Uray. Oddidle Odidatal Doo Dah, Doo Dah, Ooray." Yep, you got it, one sick Viking king here, for sure. A century later, Fritz, the local valley parrot, also learned to yodel, but only in German.

It was not known whether Letzal knew of JJ Eberhart's habit of cross-dressing. He would have been disturbed, as would any self-respecting, certified Viking. On another fascinating historical note, it seems that together they created the two dance routines now known as the Schottische and the very popular Virginia Reel. Neither had ever been to Virginia, but they vowed to go there someday. (Maynard has been there; he says it's nice.)

Every Friday night, the Stickitville folks would gather themselves up, travel the short distance over to Old Laffinatcha Meadows, the town founded by King Letzal, and proceed to dance their fannies off. They would eat loads of bratwurst-and-sour-pickle sandwiches, washing them down with gallons of Reindeer beer. For many years it was the most cherished of social events in the Crow Valley.

We're not sure just when the rift and the rivalry started. There were rumors that all the inbreeding taking place over in Old Laffinatcha Meadows was how it began. The split continued to grow, with lots of anger on both sides. The strain on couples who were crossing over back and forth, sometimes late at night, was particularly hard on almost everyone. Yucca dust would have helped out immensely, but they didn't know about it yet.

Some said that King Letzal fathered many children on both sides of the Crow Valley. Have I mentioned that Letzal had bushy, raging, out-of-control, long red hair and beard? It seemed that there was a disproportionate number of red-headed little boys and girls in Old Laffinatcha Meadows and in Stickitville.

Other folks saw it differently. Colonel JJ Eberhart had long, flowing blond curls that danced around and about his massive shoulders. Conversely, King Letzal wondered why there was a disproportionate number of boys and girls with long, flowing blond curls in the Crow Valley. It was going to be a fierce cow patty–tossing battle on a colossal military scale. Social unrest was spreading throughout the countryside. It would be a classic "Eric the Red" tossing between King Letzal B. Laffinatcha and Colonel JJ Eberhart — a parking lot standoff, for sure. Lemonade stands, food booths and other concessions were set up at a blistering pace. Somehow all the anger subsided after a torrential rainstorm cooled things off. It was rumoured that Letzal and JJ simply went off together and spent the rest of the day pinching rocks and establishing additional rules for Shark Games.

Chapter Two

Yucca Days Festival Parade

Here we were with only three days left until the Yucca Days Festival. The purpose of our annual festival is to honor and pay tribute to the mighty yucca plant, the plant with the bright yellow-orange plume that produces the yucca dust. Without it there is no path to enlightenment, no path to truth, and therefore no justice. It also puts pot and LSD to shame — although in a pinch, when you're out of yucca dust, they will do just fine. "You betchum, Red Ryder," said Little Beaver (played by child actor Robert Blake). (Red Ryder was played by "Wild Bill Elliott," Maynard remembers.)

Everyone was eagerly anticipating the festival Barbecue Cook-Off Contest and the parade, which had grown and by now had way too many floats, bands, motorcycles, bicycles, waitresses and snake oil salesmen, along with the incredible parrot named Fritz Von Schwanstooker, who spoke only German.

It was a complete nightmare for Our Hero Billy. Jim Carl had designed a fantastic float to represent Squeaky's Pool Hall in the parade this year. The Jungle Float, as it was named, was about 40 feet long and looked a lot like the *Santa Maria*, even though he would have been okay if it looked like the *Niña* but not the *Pinta*. It was decorated in jungle-style motif, heavy with foliage and supporting six 30-foot-high flagpoles. The Six Lovely Fancy Line Dancers were to climb up and down on them during the parade. Naturally, the dancers were appropriately attired while on the float and in the parade. We care about what our kids and other sensitive persons are exposed to, and even Joe Bob Pickens agrees that this is a family affair. So it shall be. By the way, we have received an application for a float in next year's parade. It has been submitted by the Prudes Are Us Society. We're okay with that, absolutely.

The choreography worked out by Jim Carl and the Six Lovely Fancy Line Dancers was spectacular, to say the least. They also used local farm animals who would be wearing costumes to simulate jungle beasts. It was a challenge to get a cow to look like an elephant — or a pig, even with sprayed-on stripes, to look like a tiger. They painted the cow's hooves to look like elephant's toes. Lilly the Cow, as she was called, was particularly happy with the extra-long, fluttering and flashy eyelashes. The bright red lipstick made Lilly feel even more beautiful.

It took plenty of yucca dust to accomplish all this, as you might well imagine. After four days of trying to get Percy the pig to growl, all the SOB would do was grin and oink a lot. They were unable to get the little sheep, named Nancy, to look like a baby gorilla. Joe Bob was secretly observed eyeballing our cute little Nancy lamb pie. Interesting, of course, in that he's nearly blind, you know. ...Hmmm.

The parade route was lengthened considerably due to the huge increase in entrants. We had several high school bands participating this year, along with the Shriners, the Jaycees, the Elks Club and the Rotarians. Not to be outdone, the ladies also had the Daughters of the Mountain Pioneers and the Daughters of the Sons of the Pioneers. We know this thanks to the archives saved by cowboy actor and musician Bob Nolan.

We were all sorry that Roy and Dale Rogers couldn't make it. However, Trigger was going to be in the parade as a tribute to them. He had been stuffed many years ago at the Trusty Taxidermy Shop, so we didn't have to worry about feeding him.

Nobody could have loved Roy, Gene and Hoppy more than I did, but to tell you the truth, my favorite movie hero was a cowboy star named Lash LaRue who was always dressed in black, with his 16-foot bullwhip in hand. He would have looked fabulous in a Coyote Sportswear Western-cut, split-yoke, all-cotton, pinpoint Oxford cloth black dress shirt. Only $49.95 at fine stores everywhere.

Lash LaRue could do it all. He would have loved the yucca dust, and I'll bet he could have snapped off a bright yellow-orange yucca plume with the 16-foot-long bullwhip in his right hand while riding at a full gallop and rolling a joint with his left hand. We miss ya, Lash. You were a heck of a man.

The high school kids from Stickitville had brand new five-star band uniforms this year. A donation from some secret anonymous benefactor. Hmmm. They were state-of-the-art, high-quality — and very expensive, for sure. The main pull-on suit body was pure white with a double stripe in red on the outside of the leg from the waist to the ankle. The tunic was all red and styled to look like a concert pianist's coat with tails. Across the chest were red and blue horizontal stripes accented with large gold buttons on each side. The front piece was designed to be worn partially open or flush up to the neck.

The hat was also white and about 11 inches tall. The bill — or shade, as it is sometimes called — was a shiny red vinyl piece, solid and hard to the touch. Trimmed to circle against the hat cylinder was a strip of gold-braided rope. There was the obligatory adjustable chinstrap. On the flat surface of the hat there was a trio — a flourish, if you will — of three multi-colored feathers standing up 10 to 12 inches above the top of the hat.

To complete this ensemble, all band members would be wearing white cotton gloves. Boots would be all-white with red and blue laces. Footwear provided by Nike. It would have been by Coyote Sportswear, but they were not making boots yet.

There was an interesting sidebar to our high school band kids, in that not one of these students could play any instrument at all. Not one of them had ever had a music lesson in their lives. They did know how to get sounds out of them, but not a single recognizable tune. The band leader just let them choose whatever horn, clanger bell or drum they felt like fooling around with when they assembled.

The kids had learned how to march, sort of. They also could keep a cadence if whoever was at work banging on the drums stayed consistent. Turning the corners while marching was a problem; some would lose direction entirely, which is how several had gotten lost over the years. I think we did find all of them eventually before too many days went by. We also found their missing parents.

Our Hero Billy gave the green light to the band leader that it was okay to pass out one capsule of yucca dust to each band member 30 minutes before the start of the parade. We're pretty sure our band leader pocketed a few capsules for himself.

The Cardoza Playboys were instructed to stay late and help find any of the band members who might have gotten lost, along with some of the parents. Happens every year. Billy says it's our civic duty and obligation to locate the feeble ones and get them safely home or someplace with friendly people who might also be lost. We would always sort it out when the sun came up again.

The next major challenge was getting the floats organized and somehow in a line that wouldn't cause gridlock — or worse, the head-on crashes of years past. "Steely-Eyed" Sheriff Geisler ordered a strict rule that "no float shall exceed 70 miles per hour at any time on Main Street," especially near the children's park. The previous year, several dogs and a couple of cats had managed to get themselves run down and squashed by float drivers who were racing and obviously lost. We think they might have been slightly overdosed on yucca dust. Sheriff Eddie Wayne said it was gonna be jail time and a very large fine for anybody getting busted.

Luke the Drifter was glad he wasn't driving a float this year. So were we. Rumor had it, he passed the job over to Joe Bob. Wait a minute, hold on — we all know about his condition, right? Man's nearly blind, for crying out loud. Jim Carl offered to tow him behind the Squeaky's Pool Hall float, featuring the Six Lovely Fancy Line Dancers. The job finally went to Dr. Mikey Lamar Cook. They all felt he could learn how to drive the darn thing before the parade started. Couldn't be that hard, or could it?

Down the street, Maggie Anne had the Boogie Woogie Burger Bar all shaped up, and the server girls were looking swell in their cheerleading pom-pom outfits. It was going to be a great day in Stickitville for locals and tourists alike.

One good thing with all the rain this summer was that the mighty yucca plants were healthy and in abundance. The bright yellow-orange plumes were vibrating in unison. One could hear and feel their power. Young guys and gals were confused by their new sensations while racing around with their perfect and naturally funny friends. As a rule, older folks understood completely what was going on in their domain. However, young boys were just gonna be men — mostly pig-like. The girls, while curious, were helpful and sometimes simply shy and often silly.

The yucca dust would change all that. With plenty to go around, many enlightenment-seeking folks would experience expansion of the mind and follow the path to truth and therefore justice. Others, perhaps in a good way, would just get seriously ripped and grin themselves giddy. Go figure. The Cardoza Playboys saw it as fun; Our Hero Billy saw it as near-mass insanity. Joe Bob didn't see much of anything, because, you know, he's nearly blind.

There were going to be about 30 more floats in the parade this year over last. It was an organizing and placement nightmare. Billy discovered that the Squeaky's Pool Hall Jungle Float, featuring the Six Lovely Fancy Line Dancers, was sandwiched in between Dr. Mikey Cook's Girl Scout float and the Jehovah's Witnesses' float. Secretly, some of the line dancers said they wouldn't mind having sandwiches almost anytime, anywhere. Dancers get hungry, too — well, you know what I mean, but I digress.

Jim Carl said that it should be okay in that it would be a learning experience for the Girl Scouts. They were going to be getting their first dose of yucca dust. He said it would give them some solid ideas about professional line dancing. Right! Uh-huh! Our Hero Billy decided to leave the Girl Scouts where they were and to move the Jehovah's Witnesses' float to the rear of the parade, behind the horses and the horse poop clean-up crew guys.

Sheriff Geisler said that if the Jehovah's Witnesses started tossing out pamphlets and stuff, he would cite them for littering and have the army-trained pit bull dog-cops escort them to jail. But Billy warned Slats, Snapper and Stinky not to say "Sic 'em," as it seemed too harsh. After all, it was festival time.

Fritz Von Schwanstooker, the parrot who spoke only German, was also moved to the back of the parade. No reason was given. He didn't seem to mind.

The Boogie Woogie Burger Bar pledged to sell their burgers all weekend long for just 72 cents each, and schooners of beer for 96 cents each. Bar owner Maggie Anne was having all her customers sign a no-foul, no-harm affidavit after consuming six beers and/or six hits of yucca dust.

Girl Scout troop leader Dr. Mikey, who was Stickitville's premier lawyer and physician, said he was particularly skilled in matters of affidavits. He told Maggie Anne that he would do it "pro bono." She said it wasn't necessary to see his "pro boner." She knew it wasn't going to be anything close to Joe Bob Pickens' "pro boner." Eyes rolled and the matter was dropped, but not forgotten.

The year before, some upstanding but very loaded citizens had broken into the local National Guard motor pool. They fired up two M-16 tanks, four one-ton military half-track vehicles with mounted rocket launchers and three "tow your own" 50-caliber cannons hitched up to CJ7 Jeeps. Why, you ask? Well, they were ticked off because they hadn't been invited and thus were not allowed in the parade. They saw it as discrimination against "real patriots" and weren't going to take it.

Folks are sensitive about parades around here in Stickitville. They proceeded to blow the living baloney out of all kinds of property. They even blew the head off the statue of Colonel JJ Eberhart, our founding father dude, down at the town square. Some of the radical bunch believed the rumor that Colonel JJ was a transvestite. They didn't want no "cross-dressing, screaming, sissy boy" kinda guy holding such an esteemed position in Stickitville's history.

Eventually, all the commotion and noise from the rockets, bombs and bullets died down. The only thing that was proven was that the Colonel was definitely a cross-dresser (Maynard already knew it). We understand that a couple of his/her outfits are on display at Squeaky's Pool Hall. None were made by Coyote Sportswear, therefore no yucca plant embroidery is displayed on any of his alleged garments. A couple of the garments had the silly polo pony on the front. The Cardoza Playboys all agreed to leave it that way and moved on.

The parade always starts at 11 a.m. sharp. This year, with all the extra floats, bands and other entries, there were surely going to be delays. However, this gave everyone more time to chug twice as many schooners of beer and allowed the yucca dust to take effect. Truth and justice was everywhere — you could smell it.

The Stickitville High School Precision Marching Band kids were looking sharp in their new uniforms. Didn't really seem to matter that they couldn't play a single song at all, at least not together.

As promised, everyone had been issued a fresh capsule of yucca dust 30 minutes before the parade was due to begin. Well, the yucca dust started to kick in like clockwork. What Our Hero Billy didn't know was that the 64-member rival high school band from across the valley (that, no doubt, would be the Old Laffinatcha scoundrels), known as the Sassy Rats Kids' Band, had shown up to be in the parade. Uninvited, of course.

The jealousy sparked by the new uniforms on the Stickitville band kids quickly turned ugly, and rocks and cow patties were being launched in both directions at an escalating rate. The Sassy Rats Kids' Band members from Old Laffinatcha were a shabby-looking bunch but tough.

Thanks to quick thinking by Our Hero, a full-scale riot was avoided. Sheriff Geisler was instructed to tell the Sassy Rats Kids' Band that it was going to be fine for them to join in and march along and that all would be welcome. Right!!

The Sassy Rats Kids were told that their starting place would be around the corner and behind the Stickitville First National Bank building. When the drums and cannons fired up, signaling the start, they were to follow the Shetland ponies straight out through the trees and down the back street. They were instructed to just keep playing loudly and marching in step. The yucca dust would surely help. Yeah, right!! Uh-huh!!

Well, the cannons fired and the drums banged. The Sassy Rats Kids were happy to be marching and playing until someone realized that after trudging for a very long time, at least an hour or so, they were six miles outside of Stickitville, way out in the "Boondocks." Suddenly it got strangely quiet. Nobody out there at all. Not another float in sight, not another band blaring another non-tune. The Sassy Rats Kids had been "had" — or, as some would say, "duped." The anger was at a boiling point, and many wanted to return and kick some royal rear ends.

Their leader said he had scored a huge bag of yucca dust from Billy's truck. Hmmm. They decided to just stay and enjoy the sunset. They figured they could come back and whip some butts next year.

Some of the Sassy Rats Kids were already working on how they could come up with equally as good or even better band uniforms. A couple of the brighter kids suggested contacting Coyote Sportswear for preliminary design work. Even though they were from the other side of the valley, they all had respect for the mighty yucca plant and the magic bright yellow-orange plume. You see, these kids also desired enlightenment and knowing the path to truth and therefore justice. A few wondered where the money had come from to outfit the Stickitville band kids. Hmmm.

The rest of the parade went off without a hitch as the floats and other participants wound their way through the park and onto Main Street past the judges. They also passed the statue of Colonel JJ Eberhart, his head still blown off from last year's not so rational parade moments.

Most of the parade judges were already half-baked on yucca dust, and the others didn't even know it was parade day yet. Actually, one wonders why Joe Bob was eventually chosen to be on the podium as one of the senior officials. For heaven's sake, he's nearly blind, ya know.

The parade was a tremendous success, and the crowd just loved it. Jim Carl's Jungle Float, with the Six Lovely Fancy Line Dancers, got the crowds up on their feet, and it won first prize in the adult category. In case you missed it, all six fancy line dancers were appropriately dressed. You can almost hear the righteous head nodding taking place on church pews all over the Crow Valley.

As is the custom, the parade ended with all the floats, 75 of them, being "wagon circled," then stacked up into a pyramid shape and set on fire. The blaze lasted until late evening, with the flames licking the clouds. Gerbils were naturally licking buckets of lollipops.

Chapter Three

The Chicken and Ribs Barbecue Cook-Off

Natasha's Salvage Yard, which is where the event is always held, was all ready to go for the Chicken and Ribs Barbecue Cook-Off Contest. The stage was set, with Charlie Mack Pearlman's podium smack dead in the center as a reward for all of his previous wins. He had won the contest for the last six years in a row. If you looked closely, you could see that his podium was a bit higher than the other competitors'. Also, it was a bit closer to the edge of the stage where the judges sat. Privately, he told friends it gave him a feeling of superiority. The truth was, he could slip a piece of his barbecued chicken or a plug of pork rib to one or more of the judges — who, by the way, were as corrupt as Charlie Mack. He said it was all just in fun; besides, most of the judges were members of the esteemed Cardoza Playboys.

Charlie had his chrome-plated barbecue unit fully prepped; it was all polished up and shining. He had added red-, white- and blue-striped flags as streamers. He also had designed and would be wearing a new outfit, which I will describe in detail shortly.

Sadly, Charlie was still under investigation for alleged blatant cheating the year before by infusing yucca dust into the chicken and ribs, along with mixing it into his secret barbecue basting sauce. Since he had a patent on the sauce, no one was allowed to test it. He would go to jail for sure if caught cheating. This year, he planned to destroy the competition by secretly contaminating the sauces of the other competitors. We will have much more on this later. Charlie Mack is a driven man, and the lure of a seventh trophy was too much of a temptation to just let it pass.

Finally, it was time for the crowds of festival-goers to traipse over to the Salvage Yard to enjoy the Cook-Off and the battle of the bands. Many of the onlookers had already voted for Pearlman. He appreciated their confidence. We have noted that some of the rabble rousers were members of the Cardoza Playboys. They were supposed to be neutral — heck, they weren't even natural.

Our Hero Billy simply let it all slide and wolfed down another burger and two beers at the Boogie Woogie Burger Bar. He was trying to explain to Maggie Anne Proctor the difference between "pro bono" and "pro boner." She just wasn't getting it. "Clearly," he thought, "she's a woman in need of a gentle but thorough backseat hugging and smooching in the Studebaker at the local drive-in movie theater."

How many — oh, how many — of us "lost it" at the drive-in? We will never know. In this writer's time of exploration and girl discovery, it was a challenge just to find and claw your way through layers and layers of petticoats, thick starched bras and strange other things (you don't want to know about the strange other things... EVER!!). All of this merely to get a whisper of a touch and a feel of the much-sought-after, but usually off-limits, waist-high "granny panties," which was enough for a few of us. Some were silk, some were cotton; however, none were made by Coyote Sportswear.

Long live bikini underwear forever — thank you, Calvin.

The two local police officers, Slats O'Reilly and Snapper McCoy, said they had orders from someone to guard the Stickitville Fish Hatchery, which hadn't seen a single fish in 20 years or more. The truth is, they didn't want to get shot at by some "wacko" who didn't like cops. They each had a good supply of yucca dust to get them through the evening if need be.

Officers Slats and Snapper played Shark Games all night. Slats was faster than Snapper, but Snapper was more cunning and shark-like. Anyway, the two players wound their way through the dungeons and tunnels of the ancient, three-storey fish hatchery building, and then eventually climbed up through the turret-shaped towers and onto the rooftop, where they found a starry night to gaze upon. They fell asleep in each other's dreams. How sweet it was. ("Eh?" Maynard says. "What?")

Billy had to go looking high and low for these two yokels. Luckily for them, the noisy valley crows had awakened them in the nick of time. They received a proper scolding but kept their jobs. Back to work scraping up drunks, deadbeats, dogs, gerbils, cats and some unused yucca dust.

The Cardoza Playboys all gathered to get the Barbecue Cook-Off Contest started. They looked so sharp in their new Coyote Sportswear matching G-9 leather jackets. The large yucca plant design had been embossed and pressed in on the left side front of the jacket. It was fantastic; there was nothing like it anywhere else in the clothing industry. Not even that guy from the old polo pony company, Ralph what's-his-name, would be able to top such a design feat.

This year we had 13 entrants to challenge Charlie Mack Pearlman in his quest for a seventh win in a row. Billy had assigned Sheriff Geisler the task of catching Charlie Mack cheating. Well, our Sheriff put Stinky on stakeout duty round the clock if necessary. The deputy relied on having a good supply of yucca dust and beer to see him through this mind-numbing assignment.

Fortunately for Stinky, Darla May McIntire and Amy Jean Ruggles showed up, offering their experience and ideas on how to administer the old-fashioned mercy mission with their special deep-dimpled smiles. They took turns giving him a friendly "handy-dandy" afternoon back-rub delight, complete with a fresh tube of Dr. Cook's Slip, Grip, Wonder Lube — you know, the re-badged can of nothing more than WD-40. Such a scam; he sold it by the case. Man, what a spectacular "back rub" it was. Stinky was all smiles. Uh-huh. Right!!

All seemed in order and we were about to start the first round in this grandiose Barbecue Cook-Off. It is is a three-day event, and only the strong can or will survive.

The Cardoza Playboys wheeled out the first of many platters of pre-cut chicken parts and country-style pork ribs. Each of the contestants was required to choose, create and submit their basting sauces and recipes. This is where it was suspected that Charlie Mack would make his move to contaminate the competitors' special sauces. It was rumored that he used a mixture of gasoline and fresh pigeon poop. It definitely worked, and he'd never been caught.

Perhaps there was or had been an accomplice. Many thought it was Natasha, but she was still all laid up in the hospital from the now-famous "flight-from-the-rafters plunge moment" onto the coffee table right in the Back Room Meeting Place, back of Squeaky's Pool Hall. Jim Carl was sent to the hospital to make sure she was still there. Yep, she was still there, all 250-plus pounds of her.

Our Hero Billy thought Luke the Drifter was a possibility, or even Joe Bob Pickens. Probably not the latter, as he's nearly blind, you know. Besides, he had spent most of his time at the Boogie Woogie Burger Bar, scouting for a new squeeze to help him polish his glorious, lucky-ducky power-dance moves. There were plenty of onlookers waiting to see just what might happen. Joe Bob explained that he always liked variety in age, for sure, but was very fond of the older crowd of experienced, "middle-aged" ladies — you know, the 26- to 32-year-olds. He always clicked his teeth when teasing the bar crowd.

*　*　*

Joe Bob would usually show up at the Boogie Woogie Burger Bar mid-afternoon, following his daily workout at the gym. Funny, but the gym always seemed to fill up with men and boys also wanting to work out at the same time. He would start by strutting back and forth doing his dance routines in the locker room where the showers were. The crowds of men and women, young and old, were a daily event and suspicious, as one can imagine. Younger men stared with disbelief and admiration; older men just sighed and appeared wistful. Some of the women swooned and wished for a look, a wink and maybe a smile.

The wives and girlfriends mentioned Joe Bob Pickens' name far too often for it to be a coincidence. He was a legend. It was known but never discussed that Mayor Spunky Dan Carlson, who also ran the gym, was charging admission to use the locker room and showers at that time of day. No one complained, even though the Mayor was obviously splitting the take with Joe Bob.

There were rules, of course: No photos, camcorders or cellphones allowed in the locker room. Ticket sales were made available to no more than 30 ladies who might want to use the men's showers at that time of day. They said the water pressure was much better in the men's locker room and they were entitled to the same privileges as the men. The truth was, they just wanted a close-up look at his jumbo-style dancing and prancing footwork. A few said they would be willing to twirl and dance with Mr. Jumbo Mumbo all night, and they did.

* * *

Down at the boat dock, Sheriff Eddie adjusted his 10-gallon hat, wiped off his badge with the cuff of his sleeve and gently patted the big iron next to his hip. He was already thinking of "sweet little Darla May" and how she was always so delightful with those girlish giggles when they were on the boat.

However, he had to get back to the Barbecue Cook-Off Contest.

The stage looked very much as though it were part of a county fair, with colorful banners and flags of all sorts, large antique wagon wheels and stacked bales of hay. A massive sound system lined the periphery. The roadies were all wearing custom Coyote Sportswear outfits. This year's choice was the bright red, all-cotton, ribbed-knit jersey sweater. Of course, each had the large-size yucca plant embroidery, with the bright yellow-orange plume on the front, looking very proud and stately.

It was late afternoon and time for the train whistle to blow, signifying the startup of all the barbecue stations. Roadies appeared and fired up the "BBQs." As mentioned before, Charlie Mack had the prized champion's elevated platform space, front and center, on the raised and decorated stage.

Adjacent to the barbecue area, there were additional platforms that accommodated the various rock 'n' roll bands on the left, and the country and western bands on the right. Always scary: the hippies on one side and the redneck cowboys on the other. With plenty of yucca dust available, Our Hero Billy, Stinky and Sheriff Eddie Wayne Geisler thought we might get through the weekend with little or no rioting, rock throwing or cow patty tossing between the art forms.

With a simultaneous drumroll from each side, the Cook-Off contestants came to the stage to be individually introduced. The barbecues were lit and the roadie stagehands exited to the left. The drama continued to build as the contestants all lined up behind their grills. Each BBQ was custom-built and loaded with features that boggle the mind. You'd think that some of them were built by NASA and cost a small fortune. As the BBQs fired up one at a time, a somber but pleasant calmness fell over the crowd — a moment of respect, no doubt.

All the contestants, except Charlie Mack, were standing behind their BBQs, wearing matching white all-cotton, beefy Oxford cloth, Western-yoke shirts with two pockets. The left-side pocket flap had the smaller-size yucca plant embroidery and bright yellow-orange plume — subtle but classy, much better than that stupid polo pony that you see a lot of, right?

All that was left was the dramatic appearance of Charlie, our champion. Lights flashed, sirens blared and fireworks exploded, filling the sky. He walked out to take his place behind the elevated and desirable winner's podium, standing tall above his peers. His outfit was the most colorful anyone had ever seen. Top to bottom, he looked something like this:

It was your basic white all-cotton and lycra-stretch blend, spandex one-piece jumpsuit. The leg-stripe trim colors were, of course, red, gold and blue. A braided, three-inch-long, string-like blue fringe dangled and danced across the front and back of the Western-style split yoke. The fringe also jiggled and jangled from the flat-surfaced shoulder epaulettes. Bright red vinyl-sparkle, shiny, pointy-toed boots rose to mid-calf, featuring dark blue and white laces (a bit gay, but acceptable).

Charlie Mack's cowboy hat (shaped like Lash LaRue's) was a 20 XXXX beaver all-white felt with a smattering of red and blue sequins around the brim, sparkling in the lights. Right smack in the center of the hat's crown was the large-size yucca plant embroidery with the bright yellow-orange plume. Inside the hat was a small lithium battery that started the yucca plant pulsing to the beat of the band. Charlie strutted and pranced back and forth across the stage, just like Mick Jagger does. Mick, of course, learned it from Marjoe Gortner, the celebrated child star TV evangelist. Betcha didn't know that. Luke the Drifter knew it. Little

Beaver knew it. And Jim Carl Lillard knew it. (Maynard, obviously, knew it.)

He also wore his beautiful custom-made, dual-pistol holsters, with the three-inch-wide belt and the twin rows of bullet-holding sleeves across his back. The yucca belt buckle shimmered in the sunlight. The holsters, just below his hips, were perfect for quick-draw action. The silver-plated .38-caliber six-shooters with gleaming real pearl pistol grips flashed in rhythm with the strobe lights.

Charlie Mack's dancing, twisting and twirling across the stage always got the crowd wildly whipped up, achieving a concert-level frenzy. It was a magnificent performance, and they just loved it. They were foot-stomping, chair-throwing, hand-clapping and girl-tossing (in a respectable, safe manner, of course). Charlie leapt up to his podium to thunderous applause. This was his defining moment in the sun. He raised his arms and fired his .38-caliber pistols into the air to quiet the throbbing, restless fans. It was clearly an expression of passion and appreciation for all the pageantry that would inevitably follow.

The crowd screamed and shouted with glee, singing song parts from the Broadway musical *Oklahoma*, which was strange, because they were nowhere near Claremore or Tulsa. It was a rompin,' stompin,' all-Canadian/American tushy-wushy, gritty-witty show, for sure.

Luke the Drifter thought that Natasha, who read tarot cards along with hitting the yucca dust regularly, had said she would look into Charlie Mack's cheating, but she never did. Besides that, she was Charlie's best friend, right down there at Natasha's Salvage Yard.

Only a few wondered whether Charlie might have stolen the all-white jumpsuit from the Evel Knievel Museum in Montana — or is it Idaho? — then added the cowboy hat and epaulettes for disguise purposes.

It was tradition for the reigning champion to toss the first rib or chicken leg onto the hot, ready-to-cook barbecue. The crowd had been hushed and was awaiting the sizzling sound the meat would make as it hit the grill. Charlie Mack Pearlman was prepared to execute his solemn and sworn duty to start the contest. The air was quiet and still, without any sound except for an annoying barking dog somewhere down in the canyon. A gunshot was heard; the barking stopped.

Then, *SSSSS*, and *SSSSS*, Charlie dropped both the rib and the chicken leg onto the grill at the same time: *SSSSS*. The other contestants followed his lead: multiple *SSSSS*s.

"Let the basting begin!" someone in the crowd shouted. With a coordinated group flourish, all the ribs and chicken parts on all the BBQs were sloshed with who-knows-what in the way of this or that basting recipe. Charlie Mack used a number 14 long-handled horsehair brush with brass clamp. He grabbed and flipped the oversized tubular salt and pepper shaker as a professional bartender would do behind a bar with a bottle of whiskey. Tom Cruise was seen smiling somewhere in the crowd. He knew what it was all about.

Charlie secretly glanced from side to side to see whether or not anyone had noticed that the particulate matter coming from the salt and pepper shaker looked more like yucca dust than your typical salt and pepper. Yucca dust has a "chrome sparkle twinkle" that will reflect the light, as opposed to the bland look of ordinary salt and pepper, which can catch your nose and make you sneeze. It takes a good eye to be able to observe all of this. Right? Uh-huh.

The crowd was watching, waiting and listening for some of the contestants to fling over a few tasty chicken and rib tid-bits. All of the bits were much appreciated, but not the tids. Who wants a tid when you can have a bit? Charlie Mack snatched generous chunks of chicken and ribs from his grill, then launched them out to the crowd. Unbeknownst to the fans, the chunks were laced with the aforementioned yucca dust.

Some said this would be the year that Charlie would be found out, busted and run out of town. Others thought he should be the Mayor instead of Spunky Dan Carlson. "Old Spunk," as he was sometimes called, wasn't even a member of the esteemed Cardoza Playboys yet. We think it was because he was stingy with the handing out of locker room shower tokens at the gym.

* * *

Almost daily, the special event at the gym was a performance under colored lights featuring the bold dance moves of Joe Bob Pickens. He would just be prancing and dancing, up and down and back and forth in the shower room. Boy, did he ever love the attention. Some of the lady guests would point, whisper and occasionally gasp at Joe

Bob's twirling and twisting maneuvers. They really loved it when he skipped and hopscotched across the locker room floor. Some said he could wave his fingers over a pan of water and create a whirlpool. This writer doesn't pretend to know exactly why that's important; I just don't want to leave anything out that could be significant. (Maynard agrees — says whirlpools are obviously important.)

When Joe Bob was a teenager, he used to dress up and show off for money. He couldn't win a lot of cash at the pool table, because he was nearly blind, ya know. It was disgusting and he was glad when he gave it up for a more honorable line of work. ...Movies...? What, are you kidding me? I'm not saying which kinds of movies — just not Westerns, musicals or war movies.

Every year, the Old West Traveling Circus and Sideshow people came through Stickitville and tried to hire Joe Bob as their number one attraction. They wanted to put him inside one of those sleazy little tents so that he could show off his fashion sense and dance moves. They promised him an endless supply of rouge and red lipstick. He eventually decided, however, that this form of exhibitionism just wasn't his style; besides, he would be forced to leave his friends. Darla May McIntire would have wept openly.

* * *

Meanwhile, at the Boogie Woogie Burger Bar, the Cardoza Playboys, including Our Hero Billy, were sitting with Joe Bob, having beers and burgers. All of a sudden a loudmouthed biker gal with a lot of tummy fat rolled over to their table, looked everyone in the eye and said, "Does anyone here know a man named Joe Bob Pickens?"

They all looked at one another, and Billy stared at her cautiously and said, "I know of him — what message would you like me to deliver?" Joe Bob was of course sitting right next to Our Hero. He started to speak, when Mad Mildred (that was her name) said she had heard of his "special athleticism" and was curious. She was hoping to make an appointment and maybe get a look-see kinda visit with him. Possibly take a few pictures. She grinned a toothy smile and said she might even have to give him a kiss and a hug herself, by golly. For sure, she wanted to get pictures and an interview. She explained that she was the publisher and editor of *Bad Bitch Biker Babe* magazine.

Joe Bob just couldn't take it anymore, so he stood up and said, "You're looking at him, Honey, and believe you me, I'm the real deal. I kid you not." (As Jack Paar, host of the original "Tonight Show," used to say.)

Mad Mildred was taken aback and glared at him. Said Mildred, "You skinny little so-and-so! When I take a man into my personal world, I expect him to 'see me' and he should look like Tarzan on steroids. Give me a real man who knows how to do some hot couch smoochin,' not some wretched, skinny-boned, nearly blind phony sitting here suckin' on a beer can. Sorry I bothered all of you."

She squinted and started to leave, when Joe Bob softly said, with a twinkle in his eye, "Okay, Miss Sugar-Sweet Pie, show up and find me at the Back Room Meeting Place down at Squeaky's Pool Hall in one hour. I'll bring the yucca dust, two burgers and four beers." He clicked his teeth, smiled, turned and said, "See ya, boys. I have some heavy lifting work to do. Catch ya later."

Dr. Mikey saw his opportunity to sell a case or two of his re-badged Super-Slide Slip-Grip Wonder Lube, which was nothing more than WD-40 in disguise. He was sure Mad Mildred wanted it for her Harley-Davidson motorcycle. She paid Dr. Cook with a credit card and said it was a business expense. He gave her a receipt for tax purposes. (Maynard wonders if anyone would seriously believe that.)

After the hard work was done and the deed of the decade came to a final and satisfactory completion, Mad Mildred stumbled out to her chopper-style Harley-Davidson motorcycle rather stunned but smiling, then slowly and quietly rode out of Stickitville. For *Bad Bitch Biker Babe* magazine, she had her story, her pictures and colorful dreams that would last a lifetime.

She also got a free bright red all-cotton Coyote Sportswear sweatshirt with the yucca plant embroidery on the left side and the bright yellow-orange plume on top. She didn't even stay for the finish of the parade and the float bonfire. She also missed the Barbecue Cook-Off Contest. Sheriff Eddie Wayne Geisler made sure she got out of town. He didn't want her kind here, anyway.

After she was out of sight, the Cardoza Playboys decided to raise money and commission a bronze statue of Mildred sitting on her Harley-Davidson chopper bike. They would title this work of art "Bewildered Mad Mildred" and would place the statue next to Colonel JJ Eberhart in the town square. It would secretly be a tribute to Joe Bob

Pickens: no one, but no one, could ever match the finesse of his "magical plucky-ducky power clocker." Just ask Mad Mildred. Joe Bob had put that biker babe on the pathway to a heavenly "cruise moan." She wore that toothy smile on her face for days on end.

*　*　*

The Yucca Days Festival took on a life of its own from this point forward. Our Hero Billy was satisfied that there was a degree of safety and security, for the moment. He decided to check out the field hospital and the emergency tent, which surely would see some activity during the festival. He also wanted to shake hands and say hello to his old friend Dr. Mikey Lamar Cook.

I haven't told you much about our town's esteemed top lawyer and medical officer. There's plenty to say about him. Well, Dr. Mikey is maybe not the baddest-looking man on the block, but it isn't wise to make him angry. He has a whistling left hook that has put down many a larger man with just one punch, right here in Stickitville.

The good doctor has his own place of honor in the form of a brass plaque mounted on the bar top at the Boogie Woogie Burger Bar for beating the daylights out of four drunk motorcycle gang bullies. He broke their noses. The bikers were going to wreck Maggie Anne's burger joint, but she told them to take their sorry drunk butts back home to Old Laffinatcha Meadows.

Nobody knows exactly when or where Dr. Mikey got his medical degree — or his law degree, for that matter. Or if he actually went to medical school. He does possess a large library of videos featuring the kind of work he does. He won't let anyone else see them, as he says they are way too technical for the layperson to comprehend. I did see a video lying on his desk one time titled *Debbie Does Dallas.* Not sure what that was all about.

Dr. Mikey was on Jim Carl's side regarding the future of the Squeaky's Pool Hall parade float and got into a heated argument with officers Slats O'Reilly and Snapper McCoy over the burning of the Jungle Float. Jim Carl wanted it to be spared and to become its own stage so that the Six Lovely Fancy Line Dancers could continue working. After all, the Jungle Float had won first place in the parade contest. Joe Bob was on Jim Carl's side also, which was confusing considering that he was, well, you know, mostly blind. Officers Slats O'Reilly and Snapper McCoy said they would take it up with

Billy. So they all went over to the Boogie Woogie Burger Bar for a burger and two cheap beers.

* * *

Much had been done, much had been said, and the festival had been a success so far. Our Hero Billy seemed pleased and relieved. The parade had been a great showing of local talent in spite of, or perhaps because of, all of the yucca dust that had been consumed over the last four days. The Barbecue Cook-Off Contest was a big hit, and all were awaiting the results from the judges. Charlie Mack Pearlman was sure he had the votes and would win the Cook-Off by a landslide.

Natasha showed up in a wheelchair being pushed by Stinky in his patrol car. It was a miracle that he hadn't run over her coming down the last steep hill. It was thought that her 250-plus pounds kept her out in front of Stinky's cop-mobile; I guess she had enough momentum.

Darla May was looking forward to breaking in Sheriff Eddie's new Chris Craft Model Number 66 speedboat. He let her pick out the foam for the boat's floor and its slipcover. She selected an all-cotton print with a high thread count. The slipcover was dotted with pictures of darling little lambs calmly grazing on a mountainside. Hiding behind trees and boulders, however, were hungry, salivating wolves ready to pounce and devour the juicy and delicate little wooly mutton-choppin' cuties. The lambs wouldn't have a chance. What kind of sick-minded person had come up with this idea, you ask? ...Hmmm. Well, it was because of too many years in the clothing business, no doubt. It's a cutthroat industry that has ruined more than one creative mind, without question. Just ask Ralph, Calvin, Burt, Ferrell or Our Hero Billy. (Who's Ferrell? wonders Maynard.)

Darla May wanted breathable, smooth comfort under her lovely bottom. No all-polyester junk fabrics for this fashion-conscious babe. Didn't matter much to our "Steely-Eyed" Sheriff; he just wanted to get lucky in love again. He adored her. This time he was going to let Darla May wear the big iron on *her* hip. She agreed, but only if he would remove all the bullets. Passion gets in the way of common sense sometimes. Darla was nobody's fool. She also was anxious to try out the latest technique recently learned from Joe Bob, which he called the "sliding and smooching, upside-down couch breaker." He said it could humble, to tears of joy, the strongest of men, and to always use this technique with restraint.

At the Barbecue Cook-Off Contest, Charlie Mack was busy strutting back and forth across the stage, firing off his matched pearl-handled pistols, when the judges stood up and declared him the winner. It was his seventh win in a row. The crowd went wild, cheering and screaming "Charlie! Charlie! Charlie!" Dogs were barking, horses were whinnying, and cats were barking, as well as meowing normally. Natasha was shedding tears of joy instead of pounds of fat and nearly fell out of her wheelchair.

Charlie Mack picked up his $10,000 winner's prize. He paid off the Cardoza Playboys and handed over a nice chunk of the dough to Natasha. She, by the way, then decided to keep the salvage yard open and to build Quonset huts for distressed lesbian ladies. Amy Jean Ruggles, girl spot welder, would assist in the plan to put all this together for Natasha and to build a new place for herself as well. She had always had lesbian lady-friend tendencies, anyway. Okay by us... as if it matters.

Joe Bob sighed and secretly cleaned his secret designer tortoiseshell eyeglasses. Hmmm. He's nearly blind, ya know. ...Really? (Maynard remains suspicious.)

Chapter Four

Yucca Dust and Purple Sunsets

Now that the Yucca Days Festival was coming to a close, Spunky Dan Carlson knew it was time to run for Mayor again, but only if he was granted honorary membership in the Cardoza Playboys. He promised he would discount the price of the shower tokens at the gym for the members. He thought Joe Bob would be okay with that.

The jail was empty at this point, and the last two guys at the field hospital were all stitched up and had promised not to ever knife-fight again. Dr. Cook said for them to leave that behavior to the low-lifes over in Old Laffinatcha Meadows. Our

Hero Billy gave them coupons for burgers and two beers over at the Boogie Woogie Burger Bar. He also gave each of them black tee-shirts and two pairs of cavalry twill five-pocket jeans from Coyote Sportswear. The tee-shirts, of course, had the yucca plant embroidery with the bright yellow-orange plume on top. Their old shirts were splattered with blood. Knife fights have a tendency to do that sometimes. Besides that, they looked better and absolutely sharper in their new clothing designed by Coyote Sportswear. There is always something good about appearing respectable.

Jim Carl Lillard was able to save the Jungle Float from the bonfire. The judges agreed that the Six Lovely Fancy Line Dancers should have the opportunity to continue earning a living when they weren't working at Squeaky's Pool Hall or in the Back Room Meeting Place. The Cardoza Playboys were happy this all panned out, especially since now there were modern, high-tech video and recording devices catching the twirls, spins, knee bends, back arching and all of the rest of the vivid action in slow motion — or slo-mo, as it's known in the trade.

For the moment, Joe Bob would remain our star performer. As you must certainly know by now, no one — at least not here in Stickitville — can match the power of the man who wears Coyote Sportswear five-pocket denim jeans, which is where Joe Bob proudly warehouses his famous manly secrets and treasures.

Luke the Drifter decided he would move on and get a place in Old Laffinatcha Meadows, as it had his kind of people there. Turned out they didn't want "his kind" at all, either, and sent him packing. His departure surprised almost everyone except Carla Jo McIntire, co-owner of Blaster's Beauty Parlor. She was Darla May's identical twin sister and business partner. We haven't said much about her yet. She was the artist of the two and was busy re-creating the Texas Modern Beehive Hairstyle for the fashion-conscious ladies. She said the idea came to her in a dream after a moonbeam dancing delight on a warm yucca dust night. That we can believe. There will be more on her later.

Yep, you guessed it, you knew it was coming. You somehow knew I wouldn't let you down. Somebody was gonna try and party with the twins in a "spin the bottle" threesome. Did you think I was going to forget about this? Surely, you couldn't imagine that I would pass this up? ...Smooch with the Twins? ...Gorgeous twins? ...A spinner threesome? ...Really? ...Hmmm!!! Oh come on, now. What red-blooded man or woman hasn't fantasized about a "brain sockets explosion" with world-class, butter- and creamy-soft twins!!! Don't you lie to me now; show me some spunk here.

From what we heard, Luke holed up in a cave somewhere and was just driftin' on his share of yucca dust — no doubt searching for enlightenment, and therefore finding truth and justice.

Amy Jean, our girl spot welder, wanted to come back and help Natasha keep the salvage yard cranking. It was a girl spot welder's paradise, absolutely.

Sheriff Eddie Wayne acquired an office right next to the jail. He cleaned his six-shooter every day and shined his sheriff's badge with the five-pointed star nearly as often. He knew he looked hot in his 10-gallon cowboy hat. He wanted to fire Stinky because, well, Stinky stank.

Our Hero Billy was looking for someone to manage the Roby E. Smith Memorial Institute. He was on a quest, searching for anyone who still had enough brain cells left to run it. More on this later — lots more.

Dr. Mikey, our doctor, lawyer and Girl Scout troop leader, who was a master at "flippin' the flubber" and also knew how to "fiddle the faddle," kept up his weekly meetings at the Girl Scout hut with the lovely moms of these posty-toasty giggle kids. He liked camping trips and horseback riding. He was especially adept at helping the moms up into the saddle. It was a fine opportunity to fantasize about getting to know some of the cowgirls in an uplifting way. A few of the moms liked to stay late and help put the gear away after a long ride. Boy, could some of them put that gear away. This was where Dr. Mikey had learned the flippin'-flubber and fiddle-faddle routines — out in the horse barn. Lots of soft, freshly cut, sweet-smelling hay out there, folks. Great for star gazing from the deck off the loft.

Maggie Anne, owner of the Boogie Woogie Burger Bar, said she wanted to sell the joint and retire. The truth was, she wanted to become a nurse and work for Dr. Mikey. She had always had the hots for the probably bogus doctor and lawyer. She didn't care either way and felt he knew enough to be doing what he'd always done.

Dr. Mikey was aware of her intentions, as she booked weekly appointments at the clinic just to get herself "checked out." He said it was okay because the money was good and she actually was a very nice lady to play checkers with. It was his job, for crying out loud.

A side benefit was the growing business of selling the re-badged cases of Dr. Mikey's Super-Slide Slip-Grip Wonder Lube, a.k.a. WD-40. He wasn't sure about having a relationship with Maggie Anne, as she didn't think he should be the Girl Scout troop leader. No way was he about to give up such a time-honored and esteemed position. Stickitville Girl Scout Troop #46 needed him. At least, *he* thought so.

Officers Slats O'Reilly and Snapper McCoy decided they didn't want to work with our "Steely-Eyed" Sheriff at the jail anymore. It was because he often entertained Darla May in one of the jail cells, where they had to listen to all the racket and commotion. Darla May and the Sheriff played cards and pinched rocks all day, and it was boring because Darla May won all the time. The Sheriff thought she was a cheater, but he hadn't caught her at it yet. Officers Slats and Snapper felt he should take her back down to the new Chris Craft speedboat; that was where the comfortable foam pad and the expensive slipcover with the sweet little lambs and the hungry salivating wolves were.

So O'Reilly and McCoy begged Our Hero Billy to let them have a work space down at the Stickitville Fish Hatchery. They would even take care of some fish if asked to. Mostly they wanted to be down there because it was a great place to play Shark Games and pinch a lot of special and highly polished rocks.

Stinky became tired of being a deputy with detective status. He thought he should also be in charge of town parking. Stickitville could be a mess at times, especially during the Yucca Days Festival. The truth was, he could scam the citizens by giving them parking tickets, offering to go deliver their payments for them and then pocketing their money. He considered it a public service and was happy to oblige so that they could get on with the fun of celebrating the festival. It was a cash-only service, by the way. Hmmm!

In an enlightened (yeah, right) yucca dust moment, Stinky decided to become a "golf pro" and hit the circuit. He'd never played golf before but had seen it on TV. How hard could it be? He went to the local driving range and was promptly driven off the course. Well, it was because he stank, no doubt.

A very angry Stinky drove back to the jail, grabbed his six-shooter, his deputy badge and his hat with the bullet hole in it, then went back to the driving range and proceeded to arrest 15 golfers, under much protest. Our Hero Billy was called to the jail and just shook his head. He let them out and gave each one of them a gift certificate to the Boogie Woogie Burger Bar for a burger and two beers.

Billy also arranged for them to get free Coyote Sportswear all-cotton ribbed-knit golf sweaters with the large-size yucca embroidery on the left side and the bright yellow-orange plume on the top. They could select from 10 color choices. The town picked up the tab, and the game of golf survived to see another day.

Joe Bob was not sure what he would do for the remainder of the season. Mostly, he would just keep himself fit and his five-pocket dancing jeans always neatly starched and in working form. Said he might take a job down at the rehab center for homeless midgets. Nobody wanted to hire the nasty little food gobblers. He said he might teach them pool cleaning or cake decorating.

Then Joe Bob surprisingly scored an interview with pretty little Miss Dolly Ruth Downs, the famous midget from Playa del Rey. She was and still is a pint-size package to behold. He couldn't help but notice that she kept glancing at his legendary fitness and his sense of fashion, especially his five-pocket corduroy jeans by Coyote Sportswear. It wasn't his fault, I swear to you — he just looks that good to the ladies.

Surely Miss Dolly wouldn't attempt jumping onto the couch while fantasizing about this vibrant giant of a man leaning himself against her tiny dancer body, would she? Man oh man, she seemed ready to play "Let's hide and play a few of the good ol' Sneaky Pete games"!! ...Hmmm... It's not what you think. C'mon.

Anyway, Joe Bob got the job doing both the pool cleaning and the cake decorating at the rehab center for homeless midgets. Didn't matter much that he had never been in a pool before, much less ever cleaned one. The cake-decorating idea came from when he was in university. Joe Bob had joined a fraternity, and for his initiation night his frat brothers thought up this outrageous scheme of covering him with blankets while he was lying face up on the dining room table. His task was to remain there quietly and not move. Next, a very tall six-layer cake covered with yucca dust icing was lowered right down over the top of him, dead center. Okay, readers — stay with me on this.

His buddies invited all the hot ladies from two or three sororities over for a party to enjoy ice cream and cake. Well, to help Pickens stay awake, it was necessary for the frat brothers to read risqué and raunchy poetry to him while he dreamed away. The promise of hugging and chugging a handful of super-cute sorority babes kept him going strong.

It suddenly dawned on Joe Bob that someone might ask for a knife to cut the cake, and he became concerned about losing his "tower of power and promise." He was relieved when told that all the knives had been removed; he was safe. The cake started to disappear by the fistful.

Now, had the stupid idiots remembered to order the ice cream? Joe Bob loved ice cream and had learned to eat vast quantities of it with a near shovel-size spoon, but he wasn't sure that his fraternity buddies would realize that they needed to keep the Häagen-Dazs (or was it Ben and Jerry's?) away from his nether regions. Are you certain you want to know all of this? Some of you people will definitely want to know, but perhaps a few things are best left to the imagination.

By then, a red-headed cutie-pie with fantastic green eyes had figured out what was going on. She was delighted by the evening's creativity and offered to "lick the plate clean," as the saying goes, but since there was no plate to lick, and no more cake to eat, she just boogied on downtown and gave Joe Bob the old "sorority hot-date twisting and hugging bug hustle dance." Yup, she also gave him a goodnight French kiss. Uh-huh. Right.

*   *   *

Billy Cardoza was finally recovering from the Yucca Days Festival. He was tired but grateful about the way it had turned out — nobody killed or seriously hurt, and plenty of yucca dust left. Now things could get back to normal and he could get some rest. It was hard to digest all that had happened in those 72 hours. Much had changed hands during the weekend: yucca dust, money, donations, scams, talent, psychedelic drugs, chicken and ribs, sport cuddling and world-class smooching, and don't forget slo-mo videos.

Did I mention money? Just who in the heck paid for the brand new band uniforms? How about the cash that showed up for "Steely-Eyed" Geisler's new speedboat? Was the yucca dust free? Who paid for Stinky's van when it was towed by Pearlman Towing over to Natasha's Salvage Yard? Did the bucks come from the brown butcher paper–wrapped packages or the five matching leather suitcases stuffed with American bucks? Well, you're going to have to wait. I'm just not ready to tell you yet. Mostly because I don't know how to end this *Tales of Wonder* "Saga of Stickitville." I'll figure it out. Be patient out there. Have some yucca dust.

* * *

Our Hero Billy took off his cowboy hat and put on his Coyote Sportswear five-pocket denim jeans and his iconic all-cotton white tee-shirt, topstitched and with longer tail and the regular-size yucca plant embroidery and the bright yellow-orange plume. He took a hit of yucca dust and felt he was still moving towards the path of enlightenment, where it is promised one will find truth and therefore justice. After climbing into his restored all-black 1967 MGB roadster, Billy turned the key and rumbled the Lotus engine to life, then headed back up to the Gray Lakes Road, where all this had started a mere several days ago.

Our Hero slowly wound his way back into the Gray Lakes Canyon. Not another vehicle in sight. He was looking for the hidden side road that only a few knew about, not far from where Stinky had rolled his van earlier. Billy pulled over, got out and carefully pushed aside the brush, which hid a long-forgotten logging trail that was definitely hard to see. It would lead up to a rather large old bat cave. A good place to hide things.

Off in the distance he heard the roaring sound of a vehicle racing along the Gray Lakes Road. It was a police van blasting up the canyon road at top speed, with red lights flashing and siren screaming, and going way too fast, even for safe conditions. My God! It was Stinky. You would think he'd know that this was not a good place to drive flat-out. He roared on past Our Hero Billy and disappeared from sight and eventually sound.

Cardoza went about his business, constantly looking over his shoulder, and then climbed up on a rock high above the cave and the Gray Lakes Road. He waited for the inevitable. After about 20 minutes he heard the police van roaring back down the hill. He sat and watched for the tell-tale explosion of rocks, dirt and dust being flung into the air once more. Yep, it was Stinky, alright. He had rolled the police van down into the same ravine as where he had crashed before. This was one really stupid hippie.

This time Billy called for emergency backup, making his way once more down into the ravine to save

Stinky's worthless red-headed rear end. The van was still mostly upright. The hippie-turned-deputy was out like a light again. The biggest surprise ever was what Billy found inside the vehicle this time. Handcuffed, gagged and still belted in their seats were officers Slats O'Reilly and Snapper McCoy. Neither could speak; they were plenty scared but not hurt.

What was also an amazing sight to Our Hero was that officers O'Reilly and McCoy were both wearing identical iconic all-cotton, white Coyote Sportswear tee-shirts. They were exactly the same as Billy's. This was one fine tee-shirt, folks. "You betchum," said Little Beaver. (Maynard is checking with Ralph about all of this.)

Stinky burped and belched, just to let us know that he hadn't yet bought the farm.

Our Hero Billy turned it all over to the emergency crew and headed back to Stickitville, where he had an appointment with Maggie Anne Proctor at the Boogie Woogie Burger Bar. Later they would all go over to Squeaky's Pool Hall for a visit, before adjourning to the Back Room Meeting Place to see if there was anything to watch on the slo-mo channel. On tap that evening on one of the regular networks was the sequel to the great movie *Field of Dreams* and its famous line about "If you build it, they will come." The sequel's title was *Field of Lollipops.* Remember: "If you plant them, the gerbils will lick 'em." (Maynard and his actor buddy Kevin have always liked lollipops.)

* * *

Stay tuned for Part Two and the continuing adventures in Stickitville with Our Hero Billy and the Cardoza Playboys in the upcoming "Rowdy Rodeo Days Extravaganza." Coming right up for you, folks.

Part Two

Rowdy Rodeo Days Extravaganza

Chapter Five

The Evolution of Vicious Viking Underwear

I couldn't agree more that some, if not most, men are pigs and that women are simply not. The ladies easily win, hands down. I am really glad for that, and here's why: Even today, men will often reach around to their backsides and scratch their butts until their eyes glaze over, with absolutely no regard as to where they are or who might be watching. It could be on the lawn out front after church, at work around the water cooler, on the street waiting for a light change or over at Grandma's house. Men will do it almost anywhere, and shame on us for not cleaning that up. It's disgusting.

You will never, never, ever, ever see women scratch their fannies in public. They just don't do it. For that, this writer is eternally grateful, along with millions of others who have a little class. So come on, guys — go behind a tree, the way you do when you absolutely have to take a leak. Or stand outside the passenger door of your buddy's car next to the boulevard, where of course no one will notice, except the kids on the school playground. Or you could walk the 20 feet or so to the gas station and use the bathroom. Is that so hard?

Alright, we are moving on now. Let's discuss this very important issue concerning men's and women's undergarments. "Panties and skivvies," as they are referred to in much of the educated world, are our next subject. They are a basic concept where women might be concerned, but to men they're sometimes an area of great mystery and illusion. It's a huge topic, as we shall see. These garments are both personal and practical considering the commercial aspects of these delicate, and often delightful, bottom covers.

In reviewing the various product realities, we see a tremendous offering in models and styles. With worldwide exposure to massive inventories, the undergarment industry represents billions of dollars in sales annually. One can trace the growth of this business, which is rich in history, back to medieval times.

In the old days, both men and women wore what was called "sackcloth" underwear — very scratchy and irritating to the touch. Nonetheless, it was a hearty, breathable yarn. It had to be miserable to wear in hot weather; we suspect that many people simply went *sans* underpants during that era. The skin rashes that plagued people in those dark times were Biblical in scope and intensity. They crazed entire populations. It's possible that sackcloth also gave rise to thousands of severely bow-legged men due to the severe chafing while simply walking. This writer will not be drawn into why more than a few women ended up bow-legged, as well. I leave that to the reader.

Skin creams and other remedies were not available back then, so they sometimes just used renderings from boiled animal fat. A product called Wonder Fat Salve would be slathered on to the affected area, but a million, billion, zillion flies would show up after each application. This problem triggered the invention of the fly swatter. A variety of styles of fly whackers and bats were designed — everyone had one or more of these new-fangled weapons.

History suggests that credit for the device should go to the Vikings, in particular King Letzal B. Laffinatcha, but we can't prove it. Yucca dust would have been a blessing during these times.

The dreaded sackcloth was hard to tailor; generally, it was fitted loosely and was available in only one color. Not much fashion going on here yet. Given the scratchy and prickly nature of the cloth, this could possibly be the reason men still scratch away with complete abandonment of any and all accepted social graces. This writer suspects that DNA plays a role in this case. Women, somehow, were able to move on, sidestep the problem and overcome the nature of the beast. We remain grateful.

Some historians say that wars between nations were more violent during the miserable "Sackcloth Period." Many a brave Viking lost his life when stopping to scratch the annoying itching while in the middle of catapult loading, spear throwing and sword thrusting. Ya gotta pay attention here, right? Scratch one, pearl two. Reload.

A wondrous breakthrough was at hand and would soon eliminate the scourge of sackcloth underwear for good. One must acknowledge the clever and ingenious Egyptians for the development of fine cottons. To this day, the planet enjoys the comfort and smooth texture of the cloth. It is a joy to touch and wear. The "silky hand" and high thread count will endure forever. Egyptian cottons are fabulous, whether they are in woven or in knit form.

Kings, queens, pharaohs and slaves praised this civilization-changing miracle cloth. Imagine — a world without crotch rot, chronic inner-thigh rash and butt-crack infestation. It simply freed up the very soul of mankind. A similar variety of cotton is grown in Arizona, called pima cotton. Our appreciation goes to the Pima Indians for this fine cloth. "You betchum, Red Ryder," said Little Beaver, who was actually a Navajo.

Because of this magical development in the textile industry, men and women everywhere became closer and more desirable to one another. No more sackcloth to offend the senses — we now had a really fine and sensual-to-the-touch fabric we call "silky cotton." Designers went crazy with their imaginations. For men, it was mostly white cotton briefs or boxers. That was really all they cared about in the early days.

Eventually, guys were amazed and delighted when some genius invented a "fumble for it" feature on all the undershorts. It was a magical, multi-layered, open-and-close envelope-type front. This was an innovation that allowed men to relieve themselves into the sunset with a smile and a sigh. Newer styles with buttons or snaps controlled the opening so that any errant, curious and/or adventurous "creeper" from the dark side would not slip out accidentally, just to say "Howdy."

The women's fashions and styles flourished, as would be expected. The miracle fabrics were cherished. Women, naturally, took very good care of their undergarments. Men, being pigs, would change them out when they got a little too "crisp" or were suffering too much from the dreaded "skid mark plague."

Models, colors and textures were explored to the max and then some. Just ask Max. Lingerie shops blossomed everywhere on the planet. Available in the marketplace were full-on pull-up waist-high granny panties, hip riders, low-slingers and something close to a modern thong. There were the decorated types with eyelet trims, waistband treatments and lovely prints — some with butterflies, some with ladybugs, some with cartoon characters; none with old maids or witches.

The real excitement happened when a little-known designer named Calvin (a name with medieval roots) came up with a phenomenal creation known as bikini panties. It was a cultural game changer, for sure. It was "New Wave," it was "New World Order," it was "New Car Smell," it was "Nuevo Laredo."

This writer wants to extend a thank you to Mr. Klein. My first experience and mind-expanding episode of the bikini adventures took place at the drive-in movie theater in the back seat of Dad's 1951 Buick Roadmaster. Thanks, Dad, and thanks, General Motors, for all the room. "Cars with couches" is what we called them. Oh yeah, many thanks to Rachel and her sister Meg. See ya at the reunion?

The next advance, which happened at around the same time, was the development of silk. Mostly, it came from the Far East, with China being the big producer, along with India and Japan. Initially, only the rich and politically powerful had access to this unique fabric. Silk is not grown from the earth like cotton but harvested from silkworms. Under penalty of death to the worms, each one has to spin out 300 yards a day of raw silk filament, or it's curtains for Mr. Wiggly Worm.

Years before, the Chinese used the worms only as a food source. This was met with limited success because when they would put them on the barbecue, most of them would just slide through the grill and get fried to a crisp. Fingers were burned by the thousands in attempts to salvage the little critters; a solution clearly had to be found.

They could have used Charlie Mack Pearlman's expertise to show 'em how it could be done. Yucca dust and molasses would have bonded the worms together and made delicious silkworm patties, sausages and burritos. It would have also made great taco meat. Or you might prefer kow loon chow mein or ju ji wonton, or maybe plain old egg foo yung. This writer would advise making sure that the worms are all dead, as you wouldn't want to see one of those little dudes crawling out of your taco. It would spoil your date with Peggy Sue — silk or no silk. "You betchum," said Little Beaver. (Alright, alright, I get it, says Maynard.)

A traveling salesman and writer known as Marco Polo, along with his brother "Ralph," struck it rich with the likes of Cleopatra McMillan and Bobby Marc Anthony. Armies of Roman soldiers guarded the famous Silk Road. It was very smooth — just like the silk undies were and are. Boy oh boy, and double oh boy. "Silk to the touch" is a delightful description.

Sensitive men discovered early on the pleasures of the luxurious feel of silk — or the *hand*, as it is called in the clothing trade. Of course, this didn't stop or sway the ruffians, bums, derelicts, thugs, moochers and perverts from liking the way it felt, also.

It has been said that in some cultured groups, the savvy women found out they could possibly catch a mate by simply wearing silk panties. We don't believe that for a second. We do believe they got attention more often, but we don't have reliable data on that.

In Barcelona, a very smart spinsterish-looking woman opened up a ladies' fashion boutique that later became a successful chain of lingerie shops called Lovely Juanita's. It was the world's first lingerie franchise, and that's no "Secret" there, Miss Victoria.

In the '50s, financial gurus advised all of us that the best way to invest our cash was to buy stock in the new miracle yarns known as the "unnatural fabrics" — specifically all-polyester wovens and knits, so named after a young and quite beautiful lingerie model known to her friends as Polly Louise Ester.

Lovely Miss Polly was from Myrtle Beach, South Carolina, and later moved to Manitoba, Canada, where she was attacked and eaten by a polar bear while ice skating near the airport one day. All that was left was her cream-colored bikini underwear with contrast eyelet lace trim and her muskrat-style headgear made from beaver fur. The panties and fur hat are there on display at the Klein Museum, which is a converted airplane hangar, along with her picture and the stuffed polar bear. Hans and Geppetto flew in to do the taxidermy on the bear. Sadly, there wasn't enough left of Miss Polly to even taxi her dermy.

Sometime later on, the underpants industry evolved to give us rayon, a product developed as a synthetic version of silk. Many involved were amazed to learn, as data was collected on this awful new yarn, that no problems were observed or became apparent during the testing. At least not right away. It seems that the wear-testing period normally allotted for new fabrics was overlooked or simply ignored.

The Pantie Police, under the guidance of Our Hero Billy, were called in to investigate. There were alleged problems that had surfaced due to a lack of product control. Several instances and complaints regarding defects had gone unanswered. Samples were therefore randomly selected for analysis from existing inventories far and wide. Companies who were manufacturing this new so-called miracle fabric were put on notice not to ship any more rayon products to retail stores. Online sales were also banned; "bootlegging" was becoming rampant; and the FPC (Federal Pantie Commission) was losing money in the millions. The risk and the possibility of a recall loomed in the darkness.

Well, here's what was discovered after diligent testing and research. The rayon panties were clingy and stuck to the body of the wearer, causing high levels of heat and sweat to appear. The potential of a terrible rash developing was imminent. Ladies from all over the Crow Valley were experiencing being stuck to their underwear right here in Stickitville. Some had to sit in a bathtub loaded with Epsom salts, lemon juice and yucca dust for hours just to be able to peel them off.

The geometry and design of the knit itself was poor, and the "grid mouse" lacked technical integrity. The layperson could recognize the problem visually due to the ruffling and the sleazy touch. The worst thing that always happened was that after several washings the "flat" of the fabric (as it's called in the trade) erupted into thousands of tiny little fuzz balls the size and look of buckshot or BBs.

So, if you were at the drive-in movie theater in the back seat of a four-door 1949 Packard Silver Arrow, the following might happen. In moments of passion, those little fuzz balls could get all snarled up and in lockstep with the layers upon layers of petticoat netting. Occasionally, either a spandex or reprocessed-rubber pantie girdle might be an added obstacle. One could get lost under all of that girl stuff, which was noisy too. Sometimes it was difficult to breathe. I once had the experience of a strange but pleasant vapor wafting up from down under all that girl-wear gear, affecting the humidity, the ozone and the CO_2. I swear it smelled exactly like dandelions. What the heck was going on here?

The bottom line was that those underpants simply weren't coming off. "No way, José." It took Mount Rushmore rock-hard determination and tenacity and courage just to get to the second feature film at the drive-in movie theater. By then it was time to go to the concession shack for a Pepsi, a large buttered popcorn and a Snickers candy bar.

A crunchy walk in the gravel took your mind off most everything. It was always fun trying to find the darn car on the way back from the concession shack. If you were late getting back to the car, the buttered popcorn was going to be cold and you became a scorned, useless jerk. That was a clear signal you weren't getting any kisses that starry night — huh, Jasper.

Following the investigation, a nationwide bulletin was sent out in the form of a recall to offer a full refund for any and all rayon panties that had been purchased. Our Hero Billy was pleased with how fast this all went down. Truckloads of relief cotton and silk panties flooded the marketplace, to everyone's delight. The cost for all of this was borne by a small tax increase imposed on the drive-in movie theater industry.

Chapter Six

Extraordinary Extravaganza Mischief

The character of Freddie was created by this writer at age 8. Like many children, I too had an imaginary "friend." He was everything to me, and I got to see him every day on my walk to school. Freddie was about 10 inches tall and he dressed like a typical leprechaun. He lived in a tiny log cabin under one of the mesquite bushes that covered the vacant lot between our house and the schoolyard. If I called for him, he would come out, jump onto the winding pathway and wave a big hello. Freddie liked me very much. When I walked along through the bushes, he would always sit on my left shoulder, telling me of his great adventures and mysterious tales. He was magic, and I felt he protected me from any harm. I loved and learned a great deal from Freddie. He was my best friend.

In this current Stickitville saga, Freddie has been re-created as an updated leprechaun-looking fellow with his own style and outward appearance to fit this new story. He's still about 10 inches tall, and he's trim and very fit, as we say these days. Not bad for someone who claims to be 350 years old, give or take a few decades. His wardrobe varies between the iconic Irish leprechaun look and all the cowboy outfits he wears. All his Western togs are, of course, made by Coyote Sportswear.

We don't know, or care, who makes his leprechaun-styled clothing. Probably that Ralph guy — you know, the one who has that silly pony and a rider wearing a goofy-looking helmet and holding up a stick, or maybe it's a golf club or something. Freddie says he has at least 50 pairs of custom-made cowboy boots, all from West of the Pecos Boot Co. Freddie likes the Coyote Sportswear outfits the best because they all fit so well and make him look super-hot.

Our Freddie has the power to make himself, and anyone else, invisible anytime it suits him, which is most of the time. He does this by converting yucca dust into "poof dust." Very handy, since, as you might imagine, being only 10 inches tall can be a problem. Some folks might try to capture Freddie and turn him into a household pet. Many would give him a nice cage, I suppose; others would just outright kill him. These weirdos would no doubt take his body over to Hans, co-owner of the Trusty Taxidermy Shop, and have him stuffed.

Hans is an artist, and a master at his craft. He could stuff Freddie in such a way that you could change his outfits whenever you wanted to. With that many outfits, Freddie would have a designer's collection, and it would be worth a fortune. I do have to tell you, though, that getting the cowboy boots on and off Freddie's tiny feet would be tough.

We have to acknowledge that Coyote Sportswear would be getting its share of exposure in the public sector. Hans could "taxi your dermy" for ya, for sure, right there in the back room at the Trusty Taxidermy Shop.

As a sidebar to our story, this writer heard via the *Trashy Pipeline Gazette* news source that it was Hans the Taxidermist who stuffed Trigger, Roy Rogers' beautiful trick-riding golden palomino. Well, our sleazy little Mister Geppetto, who is

Hans's best buddy and fellow taxidermist, helped him stuff ol' Trigger up. Most of him, anyway.

That same evening many years ago, Geppetto invited his beautiful fiancée, named Molly Anne McGregor, over for dinner and asked her not to be late; he told her that he had a very big surprise for her. With great care, the gnarly taxidermist placed a gourmet tenderloin meat cut on a big silver serving platter large enough to hold a curled-up python.

Little Richard was singing "Good Golly, Miss Molly" in the background, with full orchestration and studio-quality stereo sound. A romantic song for the candlelit evening mood: "Good golly, Miss Molly, she sure liked to ball," and so on and so forth. Catchy lyrics, indeed.

Geppetto led prissy Miss Molly Anne over to the beautifully set table. He pulled back her chair like a good and proper gentleman does and sat her down. She said, "My, my, it certainly smells good in here. Whatever have you cooked up for us?" Geppetto gracefully lifted off the silver dome cover with a masterful headwaiter's sweeping flourish. A move usually known only by seasoned professionals.

Molly Anne turned white as a sheet, blinked twice and screamed out, "OH NO, TRIGGER IS DEAD!!!"

Since that evening, not much has been seen or heard about Miss Molly Anne McGregor. Someone said that she was at the drive-in movie theater in the back seat of Joe Bob Pickens' 1956 Ninety-Eight Oldsmobile Vista Cruiser. We don't know who drove the car there — certainly not Joe Bob, as he's nearly blind, you know. Later somebody mentioned that they had seen her walking down the Gray Lakes Road muttering to herself. They said it sounded as though she was saying, "It's not the same, Joe Bob, it's just not the same." She must have been talking about the phony butter that was drizzled onto the popcorn. Sure. Uh-huh.

As an added attraction to the Trusty Taxidermy Shop, it is amazing to us here in Stickitville that Geppetto looks so much like Hans. So, could Geppetto possibly be a puppet as well? We're not sure who massaged Pinocchio's wooden noggin and brought little "Pinoke" to life as an actual living boy. We're pretty sure that there was this fairy with turquoise-colored hair who caused the life spark. Her wand had a silver star on the end of it. With a wave and a dance, she spread bright sparkles into the air, giving rise to magic in the evening light.

Duplicates of the Pinocchio dolls are neatly placed around the shop. For only 60 bucks you can have your very own stuffed wooden or soft-latex doll. The dolls are available in the smooth and squeezable version or the harder, flat-sided one that has the brass elbow and knee hinges and the funny-looking, round peg shape for a nose. You can get an assortment of different fine-threaded screw-on nose lengths as needed. They are necessary for adjustments according to the lies he will tell. If you followed the story, I'm sure you'll figure it out.

By the way, I never forgave Pinocchio for lying to the old man — it just breaks your heart. What a sorry, inconsiderate jerk he was. Never, ever trust a puppet!! "You betchum, Red Ryder," said Little Beaver.

Late at night, during one of their recent starlit summer gatherings, the Cardoza Playboys snuck up quietly to Geppetto's shop, peered over the fence into his backyard and saw this trusty taxidermy wizard dancing around the firepit with several of his stuffed works of art. It seems that somehow he is still able to breathe life into the pets and dolls that have been freshly "taxied and dermied." They danced under the stars till dawn. We suspect that yucca dust was plentiful and may well have been the catalyst needed to jumpstart the "stuffies."

The Cardoza Playboys watched as the stuffed cats, dogs, barn rats, bats, snakes, donkeys, gerbils, pigs, parrots and all kinds of other icky birds frolicked around the firepit. They didn't see a single leprechaun-ish dude dressed in a Western costume designed by Coyote Sportswear. They did have a concern that one of the stuffed parrots might be our friend from the Yucca Days Festival parade who spoke only German, Fritz Von Schwanstooker. On several occasions, one or more of the stuffies stood up and hollered out *"Achtung!!"* which was followed by the smell of burnt feathers. Someone said they heard, in a clear, guttural German accent, *"Acht Skruenzee Tung You Buttaheadas!! I'manzee on Firen Forn Jesusnzchristen Sakesen!!!"* and also, *"Doost I Habben to Dooush Midt Der Vater Alizns by Myzelfin? Nein? Vel, Woodst Dou Liken to Perhapzin Massagenzee Offen Meinen Necken and Sholderzen Sominzee Timezin?"* So said the slightly singed parrot.

Clearly, Fritz Von Schwanstooker was one angry parrot. We aren't quite sure what he meant, because we don't speak German. Fritz would have given somebody "the bird" by using his gnarly middle toe. The wicked-looking appendage had a highly polished and menacing long talon attached. He kept it sharp, clean and ready to pluck your eye out.

* * *

Freddie has the power to affect any and everyone's lives, but mostly he just lets us be who we are. His favorite thing to do is to sit on the shoulder of his chosen host and check out things from that vantage point. He always chooses the left side; he likes to nuzzle that ear. Not sure why, but it has always been that way.

Once, many years ago, Freddie visited and was mentor to a very famous character known as Little Orphan Fanny. She really liked Freddie; she thought he was super-cute and cuddly. She's all grown up now and one totally hot screamin' babe. She wears a tee-shirt that simply says "WOW."

Well, it turns out that Freddie didn't like Daddy Sillybucks; however, Freddie wasn't sure if Sillybucks was her father, her brother, her lover, or just who. Little Orphan Fanny didn't know, either. It was a strange relationship, for sure. Freddie was offended by the prominent and outrageous giant gold earring that was clamped to Sillybucks' ear and big enough to hold two rolled-up, 10-inch-long linen table napkins. The unnecessary bald head was just far too shiny to look right; at least it was smooth. The man still had the potential for a full head of hair, according to our *Trashy Pipeline Gazette* news source.

Freddie also didn't like Little Orphan Fanny's dog, which she had named Handy. He was wiry to the touch; it was like petting Velcro. He also had weird ping-pong–ball eyes with no pupils, and eyelids that never shut or blinked. (Come to think of it, Little Orphan Fanny didn't have any pupils, either.) Simply put, the dog was a scary, freaky-looking mutt.

Out of curiosity, one day Little Orphan Fanny asked our 10-inch-tall micro-midget wizard, whom she called Lepo, if he'd ever been in an intimate relationship with anyone. She thought he might be lonely. Well, that question would just about blow the socks off anybody who might be considered rational, especially Freddie. Major silence filled the available airspace. We had never heard of a Leprechaun-ish character being clearly shocked out of his pointy-toe slippers before. Definitely a first.

The earth trembled and there was a series of howling wind gusts and lightning strikes, followed by huge rounds of thunderclap from the heavens. Intense moments for all. Freddie came very close to falling off Little Orphan Fanny's shoulder. Daddy Sillybucks and Handy were both stunned and couldn't speak or bark. They just stood there, mouths agape; their eyes were following the fireflies buzzing to and fro and circling around their heads without purpose or meaning.

With great composure, Freddie calmly explained to our heroine, Little Orphan Fanny, that it would not be possible for a suave and magical celestial being such as him to have that type of relationship or engage in romantic nonsense; thus, the remarkable little runt could not make love. Frankly, there was just no natural equipment for him to perform with.

You see, a leprechaun doesn't have to eat, drink, poop, sweat or pee. His life energy is provided solely by the sun, the air and "The Dark Side of the Moon." Pink Floyd obviously plays a role here (sorry, I just couldn't resist the opportunity to do that). However, Freddie does like to partake in an occasional hit of yucca dust. Well, well, well — how about that.

Little Orphan Fanny was a bit disappointed, as she wanted to offer Freddie, out of kindness, a kiss or two. She decided that a back rub would have to suffice. Have I mentioned that Little Orphan Fanny had bright red bushy hair? ...Hmmm!!

* * *

Now we return to our story. It was time for the Rowdy Rodeo Days Extravaganza in Stickitville. To begin, Freddie the leprechaun mentally flashed up his inventory of Western-style clothes to wear, all of them made by Coyote Sportswear. After the Rodeo, he would be off to Hawaii soon. He liked to pick out his hot little grass skirt collections. He also had a fabulous assortment of coconut hats to choose from. Coyote Sportswear didn't design any of that, but would have, if asked.

For Rowdy Rodeo Days, Freddie commissioned Coyote Sportswear to re-create for him one-of-a-kind duplicates of outfits worn by our cowboy movie heroes. Of course, that would be Roy Rogers, Gene Autry, Hopalong Cassidy, Gabby Hayes and my favorite, Lash LaRue. There are a few other stars I would like to mention at this time — heroes, for sure: John Wayne, Robert Redford, Paul Newman, Clayton Moore as the Lone Ranger, Jay Silverheels as Tonto, Monty Hale, Jimmy Wakely, Alan Ladd as Shane, Rex Allen and Eddie Dean. We must not forget Bob Nolan and the Sons of the Pioneers.

Later on, we had Richard Boone as Paladin in "Have Gun — Will Travel"; along with the "Gunsmoke" gang — James Arness as Marshal Matt Dillon, Ken Curtis as Festus Hagen and Burt Reynolds as the half-breed blacksmith, Quint Asper; Lorne Greene as Ben Cartwright, with Purnell Roberts, Dan Blocker and Michael Landon as Ben's sons — Adam, Hoss and Little Joe — in "Bonanza"; and Clint Eastwood as Rowdy Yates in "Rawhide." Ya gotta remember Steve McQueen as Josh Randall in "Wanted Dead or Alive."

I would be very remiss if I didn't acknowledge the cowgirl actresses in these movies and TV series: Dale Evans, Roy's wife; Annie Oakley, the trick-shot rider in the Buffalo Bill Rodeo Show; Amanda Blake as Miss Kitty, who was Marshal Dillon's squeeze; Belle Star as the lady outlaw; Etta Place, Butch Cassidy's playmate; Katy Jurado, who acted with Anthony Quinn and Randolph Scott; Marlene Dietrich with Jimmy Stewart; Jane Russell with Bob Hope; and Raquel Welch, who starred with mostly everybody. We must not leave out Judy Canova, who starred with Hopalong Cassidy and Mickey Rooney; or Kim Darby alongside John Wayne and Glen Campbell in *True Grit*.

* * *

Stickitville was in a quieter mode now, much nicer than during the Yucca Days Festival a few weeks before. Our Hero Billy had finally been able to get some rest, but that certainly wouldn't last. The same crazy people still lived here, and they weren't going to slow down for very long. With a steady supply of yucca dust, folks would stay energized — scheming, planning and dreaming. Ongoing in our valley was the honorable search for enlightenment and therefore discovering truth and justice, an endless quest taking place in Stickitville.

Billy and the esteemed Cardoza Playboys were in meetings up to their ears. It was time to get ready for the Rowdy Rodeo Days Extravaganza. They needed to set up the food booths, refurbish the bandstands, repaint the bathrooms, then sweep the parking lots and erect the field hospital that would be next to the new outdoor car wash, where you could get a top-notch wet tee-shirt super-wash from the Girl Scout troop.

Dr. Mikey was in charge of setting up and breaking in the new car wash; he wouldn't even go for lunch. He was simply a dedicated man sitting in a lawn chair with a garden hose in his hands, just a-washing those cars. Yep, that's what he was doing. Uh-huh. Right. "You betchum, Red Ryder," said Little Beaver.

The Playboys decided to redo the helicopter pad. "Steely-Eyed" Sheriff Eddie wondered why, because the previous year, somebody had taken off in the darn thing and it hadn't been seen or heard from since. The last person we knew of using the 'copter was Luke the Drifter. He swore it wasn't him and was quite sure it was Natasha. Rumor had it that she had crashed it into the municipal swimming pool. Not surprisingly, just across the valley in Old Laffinatcha Meadows, citizens were angry because it apparently killed all the fish and nine turtles. I guess it was a mess to clean up.

Others maintained that it was police officers Slats O'Reilly and Snapper McCoy who had crashed the 'copter while playing Shark Games. Even Fritz Von Schwanstooker, the German parrot, was irritated because he too liked to go on the sightseeing trips. He cursed them — in German, of course.

Dr. Mikey had a new bunch of Girl Scouts to attend to, as they would be helpful for working in the parking lots, showing off their new summer outfits. The older Girl Scouts had the task of filling capsules with the newly harvested batch of yucca dust.

This year, it was going to cost $8 to park. That entitled the rodeo patrons to get a free six-colour poster, a brochure, a calendar and several hits of yucca dust. The poster featured Joe Bob Pickens wearing a cowboy hat, boots and hot pink shorts. In bold print across the top, it said, "Welcome to Rowdy Rodeo Days Extravaganza." Below that was Joe Bob's picture. Across the bottom, in large letters, were the words "Ride 'em, cowboy." Joe Bob seemed to be trying his best to keep his naturally shy mannerisms hiding out in the spiffy pink shorts. His massive physique was ridiculously obvious and laughable. The poster evidently caused much blushing, swooning, wishing and finger pointing.

One of the wonderful ladies, adored by everyone, who lives here in Stickitville is Golda Fitzmeyer. She's a bright, lovely and very friendly Jewish woman who owns a bistro called the Sweet Pickle and Fine Deli Meats Salon. Every time she looked at the Joe Bob Rodeo Days poster, she got the urge to break out singing, with star-quality passion, great arias from the famous classic Italian opera *Oh My Salami!* — "It means so much to me, La La La," and so forth and so on. It was truly a collector's poster for the ages. Additional prints had been ordered but were backlogged.

Over at the arena, the corral was hastily built to hold all the rodeo animals. This year we would have 56 bronc-riding horses, 27 Brahma-riding bulls, nine peacocks, eight goats and assorted gerbils. So far we only had one calf to use for both "ropin'" and "bull doggin.'" Hundreds of pigeons flew over the area because the anxious bird patrol wouldn't stay in the corral. Common barn pigeons are not trainable.

Stinky, our hippie deputy, was assigned to run security, along with the parrot, Fritz Von Schwanstooker, who would curse at the penned-up animals in German. Stinky secretly wanted to zap the parrot and wondered if he would be good to eat. "Ah, fricassee of parrot," he mused. Fritz was no "stoopnagle"; he was onto him and kept his distance. "Curses," thought Stinky.

Maggie Anne Proctor, as you know, owns the Boogie Woogie Burger Bar; she was updating her menu for the Rowdy Rodeo Days Extravaganza. She said she had learned how to make delicious tacos from a blend of lean hamburger and shredded gerbil meat. The gerbils were plentiful and a big nuisance, anyway. She paid Stinky to trap them for her; $1.70 each is what she paid him per gerbil, a bit more for the chubby ones. After skinning them out, she merely dropped them into the commercial-size kitchen blender — toenails, teeth, eyeballs, bones and all. It was about a 50:50 ratio of mixed meats. Weird, but nutritious. She added chopped jalapeño peppers, onion, cheese and garlic. She would also add half a glass of cheap red wine. (This was good stuff, said Maynard.)

The combo plate was three tacos, which included chips and salsa and your choice of black, red or spicy pinto beans. All this for just $9.84. Both Our Hero Billy and "Steely-Eyed" Sheriff Eddie were pretty sure this dish wasn't legal. "Ya think?" However, it all tasted so good that they agreed to just look the other way.

The Health Department food inspectors had ignored the severe and non-stop cursing suffered from Fritz the parrot on their last visit — all in German, of course. They had left, but not before wolfing down an order of the famous Boogie Woogie Taco Plate, and taking one order to go.

Jim Carl, owner of Squeaky's Pool Hall and the Back Room Meeting Place, had the pool tables re-covered and built a new dance floor for the Six Lovely Fancy Line Dancers. They needed to be ready to do the slap-toe trot, the jitterbug, the speed waltz and line dancing as part of their performance for the soon-to-be-here, always-ready-to-party cowboy and cowgirl crowd.

Jim Carl had begged Amy Jean to come back to work at the Back Room Meeting Place, offering to double her salary. The Cardoza Playboys were thrilled that sweet Amy Jean, with her wonder-smile and off-the-charts knuckle-deep dimples, was maybe coming back. Jim Carl said he would give her plenty of time to help Natasha build the Quonset huts for the distressed and lost lesbian gals.

Meanwhile, Charlie Mack was still basking in the sun over his seventh straight win at the Barbecue Cook-Off Contest. He didn't know if he'd try for the eighth win next year. Traces of pigeon poop and gasoline had been taken by investigators from the trunk of his all-black Hummer SR-4. He was waiting on the lab test results, which had been sent off to the Capital Contaminant Processing Plant in Washington, DC. There continued to be a lingering suspicion that he had simply cheated.

Spunky Dan Carlson was elected Mayor for another six years. Prices for shower room tokens at the gym remained artificially high but sold out nevertheless. Identical twins Darla May and Carla Jo McIntire continued in business as the owners of Blaster's Beauty Shop. We were still not totally sure about the upcoming slo-mo video regarding the threesome. Well, this writer has kind of promised, right? The twins demanded to be allowed to have their hair done up in the newest style of the modern Texas Beehive Deluxe Super-Curl Spin. This was contingent on whether or not it was to be filmed.

Meanwhile, something silent, sinister and top-secret was taking place over at Old Laffinatcha Meadows. The eons of strife, rivalry and jealousy had continued in sort of a smoldering limbo. A historical phenomenon was unfolding, and no one could have anticipated what was about to happen.

A handsome young man, probably in his mid-20s, was sitting in the living room of an old restored cabin, drinking a Reindeer beer and finishing off a bratwurst-and-sour-pickle sandwich. The cabin was near the cave where King Letzal B. Laffinatcha's hot-air balloon had crashed over a century ago.

The young stranger was tall — about six-foot four — and lean but muscular, with a predator's controlling and piercing blue irises pasted on top of the wet and shiny porcelain whites of his eyeballs. And his hair!! Oh my, his hair was bright red and bushy. It was the texture and volume of six woven Brillo pads. All of a sudden, adding to this scene, his identical twin brother stepped from the den and stood in the doorway. The two were, without a doubt, direct descendants of King Letzal

B. Laffinatcha and were widely known as Prince Imagona B. Laffinatcha and Prince Wergona B. Laffinatcha. There will be much more on this stunning revelation. Perhaps all of this will evolve in a way that this writer isn't completely sure of, yet. Stay tuned.

Some of you are prepared and ready for an all-out war between Stickitville and Old Laffinatcha Meadows. But will the threesome now be a foursome? Excuse me, are we talking golf here or something else entirely? We really need to think about this, folks. My, oh my. Golf, or group Tiddlywinks!! What's it gonna be? (Maybe we should check with Maynard.)

Chapter Seven

Ralph's Six Dirty Bandits

After long and intense meetings, the Cardoza Playboys were stronger than ever and were eager for the Rowdy Rodeo Days Extravaganza to begin. Several more meetings continued to take place, to set up this year's rodeo event. Mayor Spunky Dan Carlson was looking for ways to raise revenues in order to cover higher costs. He set up suggestion boxes over at Squeaky's Pool Hall and at the Boogie Woogie Burger Bar.

Last year a lot of cash was raised by offering hot-air balloon rides. They had 12 balloons coming and going all day and night. At the end of the Rowdy Rodeo Days Extravaganza, we actually got seven of them back. Search-and-rescue airplanes, foot patrols and sniffer dogs are still looking for the other five.

Sheriff Eddie Wayne Geisler reassigned Fritz Von Schwanstooker to the care of the Cardoza Playboys. Things were getting tense, out of hand and clearly much too dangerous to leave the parrot with Stinky. Besides that, Fritz was allowed to hang out with the Playboys. He would curse almost any and everything he didn't like — in German, of course. He was a plush, pushy parrot on a power trip.

To increase security over last year, it was decided that Stickitville should have its own independent horse-mounted posse. Its membership was composed of our usual local screw-ups, including the Playboys and officers Slats O'Reilly and Snapper McCoy. Jim Carl Lillard was voted in as Captain of the new organization.

This gaggle of misfits called themselves the Dusty Bunch. All members of the Dusty Bunch posse were outfitted in black long-sleeved, cut-and-sewn, 100-percent cotton twill sport shirts with the yucca plant boldly embroidered on the left side and the yellow-orange plume on top. They chose the large-size embroidery. It was about three inches tall. There were no pockets on this shirt model.

The yucca logo was visually strong in appearance and very handsome on the black background. All clothing was, of course, developed by Coyote Sportswear.

Each shirt was styled with the classic front-and-rear-split Western yoke and had pearl snaps instead of buttons. The boot-cut jeans were worn with a black three-inch-wide Western-style leather belt fitted with a large silver buckle. The Dusty Bunch signature inlay was etched in on its face, and solid gold rope trim stretched around the buckle's edges. Yucca plants with the yellow-orange plume were spaced out and tooled into the leather. As well, each member had their first name centered and tooled in on the back side of the belt.

All riders in the posse wore black all-cotton denim five-pocket jeans. Their cowboy boots were black shell cordovan leather with a pointy-style toe and a three-inch-high slanted heel. Captain Lillard's boots had a solid silver toe-piece overlay, signifying his leadership position.

Also as part of their outfits, the Dusty Bunch members wore black felt cowboy hats with a silver star mounted on the front. Captain Jim Carl's cowboy hat was white felt with a gold star on the front. It was all about style, position, rank and more. The presentation totally reflected the Western look and fit in with the Rowdy Rodeo Days Extravaganza and its many traditions.

In addition, the Coyote Sportswear Western design division was asked to create an all-leather motorcycle gang–type vest. On the back side, it had the Dusty Bunch logo embossed around the semicircle top, all in red letters. Just below center were the words "Rowdy Rodeo" done in orange. Above the orange "Rowdy Rodeo" was the full-size yucca plant with the yellow-orange plume. Next, embossed on the welted back strap across the bottom, were the words and numbers "Stickitville 2019" in white letters. All open seams on the vest were closed with quarter-inch-wide saddle lacing. Our parrot Fritz Von Schwanstooker was thrilled at the possibility of getting a motorcycle gang vest. The entire collection was awaiting approval from Our Hero Billy.

What might stand out as odd to you, the readers, is that I haven't told you yet what's next on our journey in the Crow Valley and in the ongoing "Saga of Stickitville." Relax. Have another toke.

There were a total of 13 posse members, plus officers Slats O'Reilly and Snapper McCoy, as they were already employees and certified police officers. All male riders would be assigned identical pure, solid black thoroughbred stallions. Captain Lillard's horse had a small white blaze on its face that looked strangely like an electric hip-hop version of the yucca plant. Imagine that.

I should make note right here that our posse had a unique stand-alone feature in its membership. Officer Snapper McCoy would not be on a horse. He would be riding patrol from a distance of 30 yards at the rear of the posse. His ride: a red 1948 Cushman Road King motor scooter with a two-speed side shifter. Yep, there was a reason for all of this. Stay with me; I will "esplain" it to you, as Ricky Ricardo used to say to Lucy.

Most of you probably saw Mel Brooks' huge movie hit *Young Frankenstein*. If you didn't, then do so. It is seriously funny. One of his characters was named Frau Blücher; she was the keeper and matron of Dr. Frankenstein's evil-deeds castle and was played masterfully by Cloris Leachman. Each time her character's name was spoken in the movie, any and all horses in the area would panic and whinny in fear. Simply hearing the sound of her name would cause the horses to buck, twist and jerk. They would rear up with their front legs frantically pawing the air. Then they would try and escape to anywhere just to get away from Frau Blücher. It was hilarious and always got huge laughs from the audience. She was mysterious and sinister. She also played morbid and depressing songs on her violin.

Well, it seems that Officer Snapper McCoy has the same strange personality trait as Frau Blücher. We think it's in his DNA. When he showed up, the horses would go bonkers to completely nuts. The Dusty Bunch all wanted Snapper to be in the posse, so they said he could be, as long as he rode his treasured red 1948 Cushman Road King motor scooter with the two-speed side shifter and stayed at least 30 yards back. Officer McCoy agreed, provided he too was allowed to wear the Dusty Bunch posse's motorcycle gang leather vest.

It was also decided that the parrot, Fritz Von Schwanstooker, would accompany Officer McCoy on patrol. He would perch on the handlebars of the Road King scooter and guide Snapper by pointing his outstretched wing and leaning in the same direction as the Cushman on each and every turn. He became a pro in no time.

A cowboy hat didn't look right on Fritz, so they found him a WW II shearling-lined leather fighter pilot's aviator cap with side flaps. They also found a pair of teardrop-shaped goggles to cover his huge parrot eyes. Yep, he got a much-desired Dusty Bunch leather motorcycle gang vest as well. He was one arrogant goose-stepping parrot. He would curse at the black stallions galloping out in front or at anybody else who got in his way, shouting out — in German, of course — *"Movinzee Yers Dummkopfs Fatinzee Asses, Schtupid Buttafazes. Gidden Zeeupin Youse Jerkin-Zeeoffins Mudder Schmukkers!!!"*

Officer Snapper McCoy laughed so hard that on several occasions he darn near crashed the scooter. Fritz didn't think it was funny. He cursed Snapper and thought he shouldn't be driving. Fritz thought that Officer McCoy should sit on the handlebars instead.

Remember now, our Officer Snapper McCoy looks a lot like Danny DeVito. Is it getting funnier yet? I hope so, 'cause this stuff isn't easy to do. Back to the saga.

Saga Alert!!! Saga Alert!!!

One new development surfaced that needs to be addressed right now. Billy decreed that women would be allowed to be part of the Dusty Bunch posse. A rush was implemented to get their outfits designed and made in time for the Rowdy Rodeo Days Extravaganza parade.

Some restrictions would apply for this first year. There would be only two ladies chosen for the posse because of time constraints. Our Hero, along with the Cardoza Playboys, selected the identical twins Darla May and Carla Jo. They would ride just slightly behind Captain Jim Carl, one on each side of him. Their outfits mirrored the men's, except they were color-reversed. In other words, whereas the men were in black, the women were in white. The McIntire twins' horses were identical white pure Arabians from the Vermont Horse Farms.

Captain Lillard was excited to have the twins on board. He had already secretly paid the Coyote Sportswear Western blouse designers to make sure the twins got to show off their wonderful, shapely assets. Actually, it was the twins who had come up with the idea. Their job was to carry the poles that flew the flags on parade day; this was a practical suggestion, as who was better at performing in formation than these two, anyway? The Cardoza Playboys wanted the lady posse members to have their own identity. They wanted the gals to call themselves the Trusty Dusty Pussycat Posse. ...Purr. And meow.

Jim Carl called a meeting to practise the upcoming but yet-to-be-learned maneuvers the posse would have to know by parade day. Then, all of a sudden, Our Hero Billy was phoned and told by Officer Slats O'Reilly that the First National Bank of Stickitville had just been robbed. The seemingly unknown crooks were headed towards the badlands just north of Old Laffinatcha Meadows. They were all on horseback — six bandits poorly dressed in worn-out cotton piqué golf shirts with a silly-looking embroidery of a stupid-looking pony and a guy holding what appeared to be a long, skinny croquet mallet above his head.

On leaving the bank, one of the "Six Dirty Bandits Gang," so named by Billy, had been heard to say, "C'mon, Ralph, we gotta whip and spur our rear ends out of here." Ralph, however, thought they had time to go over and get a couple of burgers and two beers from Maggie Anne Proctor's Boogie Woogie Burger Bar. He said that if they didn't eat something they would all be starving before nightfall.

Stickitville's esteemed posse, the Dusty Bunch, along with the Pussycat Posse, sprang into action under the direction of Our Hero Billy, Captain Jim Carl Lillard and "Steely-Eyed" Sheriff Eddie Wayne

Geisler. They were off at a full gallop, hot on the trail of those rotten bandits. Officer Snapper McCoy and Fritz the parrot were precisely 30 yards behind on the 1948 Cushman Road King scooter with the two-speed side shifter. Those crooks were really bad; they had even stolen the pension checks being held at the bank for poor widows and orphaned children all over the valley. They were "Inglorious Bastards," for sure. We did hear that Brad Pitt was flying in to join the Cardoza Playboys. We think it was just to enjoy the posse — not sure which posse. He didn't say. What do you think? (Maynard certainly knew.)

Well, even after hundreds of bullets had been fired back and forth between the Dusty Bunch posse and Ralph's Six Dirty Bandits Gang, it was still a standoff, so "Steely-Eyed" Sheriff Geisler and Captain Lillard decided to stealthily move around the large rocks and boulders, with Ralph's gang hiding right behind them, in an attempt to close the bandits off.

Officer Snapper McCoy and Fritz began circling a large oak tree while tethered 15 feet out from the tree's center. They made nine trips around on the Cushman scooter. McCoy was a-shiftin' her up and a-shiftin' her down — he was really working that two-speed side shifter. Don't know why, but it looked so funny, as they were getting hopelessly dizzy. Fritz cursed Snapper for being that stupid. *"Ver Exactingly Dus Vun Ich Finden Shuchin a Dummkopf und a Ninkompoop!!"*

So far, nobody had been hit or hurt. It had been great drama, with the wonderful sounds of bullets ricocheting off the rocks and trees. *Patoing, patang, scaabing, sproing, caaduring, zerring, splaange and ka-chinga-kaching.*

Finally, Ralph's Six Dirty Bandits Gang had had enough and gave up, on the promise of two hits of yucca dust before they would be on their way to jail. Also, they negotiated for burgers and two beers each evening from the Boogie Woogie Burger Bar.

Our Hero Billy radioed in to headquarters for a hayride wagon to be sent over to the badlands just north of Old Laffinatcha Meadows. Apparently, all of Ralph's Six Dirty Bandits' horses had taken off in a panic at the first sight of Officer McCoy and Fritz Von Schwanstooker circling the oak tree. They wanted no part of that scene. It would be several days before the horses were found grazing peacefully in a lovely grass valley near Stickitville.

The hayride wagon arrived and a rope tow was fashioned to hitch up to Officer McCoy's 1948 Road

King scooter. Snapper shifted the Cushman down a gear, then towed the bandits back to town and jail. Fritz, meanwhile, had perched himself on the top of the hayride wagon's flagpole, and he proceeded to curse Ralph and his bandit guys relentlessly all the way to Stickitville. All in German, of course. *"Didst Yousa Buttaheadus Dinka dat Yousa Kooda Robba Meinen Banken? Nosirea, Weeinzee Gonsta Dumpa Yoren Sorienzee Azzes in das Jailahaus forenzee ah Longah, Longah Timenzee."*

Ralph immediately requested a meeting with Maggie Anne to get the name of the lawyer who did work for her pro bono. Well, she would think about it, as she was still reeling over her personal discovery of enlightenment. Her recent education regarding the pro boner / pro bono misunderstanding had transformed her into a new woman. It took extra hits of yucca dust, a burger and two beers, but she finally got it. Thus, along with the enlightenment came truth and therefore justice. She also asked for, and got herself, a nice evening featuring plenty of sweet and gentle couch smooching with good ol' Dr. Mikey Lamar Cook.

At the rodeo grounds, Darla May and Carla Jo set up the booth for their company, Blaster's Beauty Shop. They would be teaching all kinds of hairstyling to the younger girls in Stickitville. The McIntire twins were really focusing on their newest project, the re-creation of the Texas Deluxe Beehive Super-Curlyspin Hairstyle. They said it was for the modern woman and looked spectacular. As for marketing, the twins could give this creation just the right sparkle and flair. They had already drawn the attention of major fashion publications. Even Mad Mildred from *Bad Bitch Biker Babe* magazine had shown interest. Upon hearing that bit of news, Joe Bob clicked his teeth and wandered over to Squeaky's Pool Hall and the Back Room Meeting Place. He said he would watch a movie if he could get a seat up close to the screen. He's nearly blind, you know.

Amy Jean Ruggles was pretty sure she would like moving back to Stickitville to help out at the salvage yard. Natasha had okayed Amy Jean's request to open a girls-only spot welders' school right there at the yard. Amy Jean would also work nights and weekends at the Back Room Meeting Place. The Cardoza Playboys were thrilled.

With the Rowdy Rodeo Days Extravaganza about to start, the news arrived that Charlie Mack Pearlman, winner of the Yucca Days Barbecue Cook-Off Contest, had been cleared of any wrongdoing in winning his seventh championship crown. Authorities had judged that there was not enough evidence to charge him with criminal intent. This writer is glad, as I know that Charlie Mack is a fine, honorable human being. So there.

Coming right in on the heels of this announcement, the Cardoza Playboys selected Charlie Mack to be the Grand Marshal for the entire Rowdy Rodeo Days Extravaganza. His duties would be as follows:

1. Organize the Rodeo parade for cowboys and cowgirls on horseback and those riding in buggies.
2. Oversee one-way hot-air balloon kiddie rides.
3. Schedule the senior ladies' cake bake and apron sale.
4. Oversee the blindfolded seniors at the turkey shoot.
5. Organize a bikini bathing suit fashion show for the Hutterite, Mennonite and Amish ladies.
6. Find judges for the fat man's pajama dancing contest.
7. Find judges for the fat woman's pajama dancing contest. (*Cannot be same judges.*)

8. Oversee trapeze and high-wire lessons for seniors.
9. Oversee cow-patty baseball game.
10. Find coaches for the seniors' nude indoor bowling championship.
11. Find counselors for the children's flaming gerbil toss.

In addition, Charlie Mack wanted the Cook-Off Contest at this Rodeo Extravaganza festival to continue to be for cheeseburgers only. He was going to allow Maggie Anne to enter in the professional category. She, of course, owns the Boogie Woogie Burger Bar. Restrictions and special rules to follow.

Captain Jim Carl called on Luke the Drifter to manage and work the salad bars and condiment stations at the Cook-Off. To keep it fair, Luke was instructed to limit the yucca dust to a low-dose additive. Ha!! He had already figured out how to load the "dust" into the blue cheese dressing and the croutons. He had tried some himself two days before; it had then taken him four hours to find his cave, which was only two blocks off Main Street. When asked about it, he said, "It's good stuff, Maynard." (Who the heck is Maynard?)

Voting for the Rodeo Queen and her court would take place right after the Fancy Line Dancing

Competition. Amy Jean Ruggles was in a league all by herself. Boy howdy!! Nobody could dance the Doo-wah Diddly quite like Amy Jean.

Charlie Mack was thrilled about being cleared of any criminal activity during the recent Yucca Days Festival. Winning his seventh straight title at the Barbecue Cook-Off Contest was a personal and highly emotional victory for him, even though quite a few old-timers rolled their eyes regarding the exoneration. In an effort to not get stuck, we were going to stick with the decision here in Stickitville, anyway.

Charlie was equally elated at being chosen Grand Marshal for the Rowdy Rodeo Days Extravaganza parade. He had planned on being Drum Major and had already made special changes to his Barbecue Cook-Off Contest uniform — you know, the one with the Evel Knievel flavor to it. The Lash LaRue 20 XXXX all-white beaver felt cowboy hat would be put on the shelf for another day. It would be replaced with a super-tall, 26-inch white shag beaver bonnet styled like the ones worn by the Queen's honor guard at Buckingham Palace. Beavers are good; but I digress.

His Grand Marshal outfit was still going to be the basic white cotton and lycra stretch spandex one-piece jumpsuit. To enhance and change the look of the jumpsuit, Charlie added shaggy white beaver wrist cuffs and 10-inch-long matching white beaver ankle cuffs. A gay look, for sure, but appropriate.

Both McIntire twins arrived, their six-shooter pistols hugging their hips in the quickdraw position. Charlie also recommended pistols for all the rest of the band members, including the 25 pom-pom girls and the eight sparkling majorettes. Marching right behind whoever got chosen as Drum Major would be the Six Lovely Fancy Line Dancers and the eight majorettes, trailed by the 25 pom-pom girls.

Following that would be the 60-piece marching band in their new uniforms. They still could not play one single tune, as there had not been any time for music lessons. So they would simply try to march in step to a regular drumbeat, blasting out whatever blaring sounds they could get from their instruments. The *clack-clack* sounds of the clanger-bells being slammed together clashed noisily with the *toot-toot, wa-wa, oompahpah* tubas and loud-shriek-whistle sounds. The slide trombones were just a-sliding and a-gliding perilously close to the overhead crash cymbal players, who were ducking as they marched.

I have forgotten to discuss Charlie Mack's battery-operated baton, which was a unique and stunning work of art. It was smooth, long and spearlike, similar to a unicorn's pointed and spiraled horn. The base, or ball, sometimes called the orb, was made from mirror-finish chrome. Only a few knew that it unscrewed so that Charlie could keep a sufficient supply of yucca dust inside. Brilliant.

This writer thought the band should have learned at least one song that they could all accomplish as a band unit. Natasha suggested a fight song, and they would have been welcome to use the one from yours truly's alma mater, which goes like this: "Onward Roswell, onward Roswell, fight until your fame, pass the ball around the field, a touchdown every time, rah rah, rah rah," and so on and so forth. What is noticeably embarrassing is the fact that our esteemed local leaders at Roswell High School thought it was perfectly okay to hijack both the lyrics and the tune from the University of Wisconsin. They just switched out the word "Wisconsin" for "Roswell," and away they went. Shameful, indeed; we could have done better than that. For example: "Cee Cee — Cee Oh Y — O Tee Tee — Tee E S — COYOTES, or KY-YOATS." Perhaps I need to do this: "See See, See Oh Why, Oh Tee Tee, Tee Eee Ess. Ky Yoates." That was a lot of work;

I won't do that again. *Boom-a-laka, boom-a-laka, sis-boom-bah.*

Many in Stickitville wanted Charlie to be Drum Major and lead the band and the rest of the entourage. This was because he was always a master showman; we have previous video of him rushing from the back row through the nine horizontal rows of band members. He would burst through the center out onto the field to tremendous applause from his fans. They were cheering, yelling, clapping and screaming, "Charlie, Charlie, Charlie!" He was high-stepping, knee-lifting, baton-pumping and whistle-blowing at lightning speed. He floated to and fro and back and forth in front of the band, which was blaring out a dream collection of non-tunes as loudly as possible. The majorettes, along with the pom-pom girls and, of course, the Six Lovely Fancy Line Dancers, were in awe of Charlie Mack Pearlman. He could always guarantee the crowd of fun seekers a spectacle of spectacles.

Charlie wrestled in his mind over just who he could choose to replace him as lead Drum Major. He considered Luke the Drifter, since they were the same size, but Luke was lazy and not very coordinated. He thought about Stinky, the hippy-dippy deputy, but that was a non-starter because he stank and the Evel Knievel suit might not ever recover. He couldn't see how Dr. Mikey or Spunky Dan Carlson would work out. They simply had no talent.

That left about three potential replacement possibilities: Jim Carl (had a bad knee), Sheriff Eddie Wayne (distracted by pretty girls) and Our Hero Billy (first choice if available). Officer Slats O'Reilly was woefully tone-deaf. We couldn't use Joe Bob, since he's nearly blind, ya know, and the girls would be disturbed anyway, knowing full well that this super-duper pussycat scooper of a man was wearing the magic Evel Knievel band uniform. In fact, any accidental tumble on the field might cause him to have to stand on one leg. Hmmm. Hard to march that way. The guy might fall down!

In a moment of humor, Charlie, who could be a very funny man at times, chuckled at the thought of maybe choosing Officer Snapper McCoy. Snapper was barely five feet tall and built like a Dallas County "fire plug" (also known as a fire hydrant), and he wore Coke bottle–thick eyeglasses. His uniform would hang off of him worse than if it was on a lost Bedouin dwarf. The bottom of the six-shooter holsters would stop at about one inch below the knee or even lower. Try and imagine the tall, shaggy white royal guard beaver hat pulled way down over his ears, and the fuzzy wrist and ankle beaver shag. The baton was several inches longer than he was tall. Snapper would like the chrome orb, however. None of the other Cardoza Playboys would work. So, if he would do it, then Our Hero Billy was definitely the first choice.

Natasha had been on the mend for a couple of weeks now. She was lucky to be alive and not permanently injured after the famous "from-the-rafters plunge" down at Squeaky's Pool Hall, in the Back Room Meeting Place. She had made up with Joe Bob and Amy Jean, and they were all friends again.

At the Rowdy Rodeo Days Extravaganza, the parade would cover both ends of the fairgrounds and pass through the downtown as well. The success of the Yucca Days Festival had caused the Rodeo Extravaganza to mushroom in popularity and become maybe even bigger than the Yucca Days event.

The traditional country lifestyle is a big deal here in Stickitville. Not surprisingly, it's also the community focus of our neighbors over in Old Laffinatcha Meadows. Surprisingly, their 64-piece Sassy Rats Kids' Band somehow came up with the money for new uniforms. Hmmm. Coyote Sportswear agreed to style up their great-looking outfits. Coyote's concept for the Sassy Rats Kids was a bold color scheme and technically forward design. The uniforms looked something like this:

The dark purple one-piece jumpsuit was made from close-cut royal velour with a satin finish and trimmed with the accent colors of teal and bright yellow. The overall look had a French fashion taste about it, as the d'Artagnan Three Musketeers–style white hat featured a single huge, bushy purple feather flowing from the side of the hat and over the left shoulder. The boa-like feather was at least 27 inches long and 13 inches in diameter at the widest point; then it tapered, very fluffy and swishy, down to zero. The jumpsuits had lacy eyelet sleeve cuffs and matching floral-style ankle cuffs. The white vinyl slip-on boots were covered in tiny yellow and purple stars. The Old Laffinatcha Meadows high school Sassy Rats Kids' Band just might have out-styled the more confident and laid-back Stickitville kids' band.

In a tribute to old King Letzal B. Laffinatcha, his descendants Prince Imagona B. and Prince Wergona B. rewrote Aerosmith's hit tune "Walk This Way," changing it to "March This Way."

The kids practised until their minds and fingers were fried. It takes a lot of yucca dust to learn a song in two weeks. It was certainly remarkable considering that not one of these kids could play anything but loud noise prior to the challenge. It was payback time for the prank pulled on the Sassy Rats Kids' Band during the Yucca Days Festival. The Stickitville kids still couldn't play a song — not even close to a tune of any sort.

In other interesting developments, Our Hero Billy had several meetings with Ralph, the leader of the Six Dirty Bandits Gang. For sure, they were a misguided bunch, but not stupid. Billy felt that if he worked the politics of Stickitville just right, he could get them a lenient probation and maybe a full pardon.

The Rowdy Rodeo Days Extravaganza desperately needed more manpower and raw talent. It was agreed upon that Ralph would be in charge of the Six Dirty Bandits Gang and would assign duties to them based on their particular skills. Ralph didn't know it yet, but he was also being considered for Drum Major. At least, they had him measured up and ordered a custom band uniform ready to go just in case.

Chapter Eight

Rowdy Rodeo Ruckus

As the start of the Rodeo Extravaganza quickly approached, it all began to take shape. Already the campgrounds were nearly full. There were pickup trucks by the hundreds and nearly as many horse trailers and motorhomes. A few of the covered wagons that would be featured in the cowboy parade were starting to show up and gather at the north end of the rodeo grounds. The hot-air balloons were fired up daily to make sure that they were all functioning properly.

Hard to imagine, but this year we would have 75 balloons, giving us serious management problems. Each morning and evening, mass ascensions were scheduled for launch. Our "Steely-Eyed" Sheriff asked the balloon pilots to limit their intake of yucca dust this time, as we were still looking for the five missing balloons from last year. To go from 12 balloons to 75 was total insanity.

The probation for the Dirty Bandits and the subsequent pardon were fast-tracked, and Ralph seemed grateful. He promised to behave and be of service to Our Hero and the surrounding communities. He said that after the Rowdy Rodeo Days Extravaganza was over, he was going to put his efforts back into designing clothes. Ralph had been working on a new logo featuring an alligator being ridden by a soccer player with a stick, or something, held above his head. We thought the folks at Lacoste might have a say about whether that idea would get any traction.

The designers at Coyote Sportswear figured that Old Retro Ralph should stay with his day job and leave the design work to those of us who understand the marketplace. Ralph said, "Widen the tie, watch the jacket makers crumble." Over a beer, he was heard mumbling something about a polo player on a horse in case the alligator idea didn't pan out. How stupid was that? Turns out it was about *Five Billion Bucks' Worth of Stupid*. Wish the folks at

Coyote Sportswear had thought of it. Oh well, the yucca plant logo was just gonna have to do.

Captain Jim Carl once again called for a practice session for the Dusty Bunch at the rodeo grounds. There was a lot to learn in order to be able to follow his commands. He wanted the precision moves executed on time and hitting their marks, with no screw-ups. A dress rehearsal was arranged for the following Thursday. The parade and kickoff for the Extravaganza was Friday. The color guard was ready and looking sharp. The international flag bearers were in customary alignment with the rodeo wranglers.

The Professional Rodeo Organization (PRO) took care of most of the work needed to run a big-time rodeo event. They did all the management tasks regarding the competitors and the rodeo animals. The arena was in great shape, with all the flags, lights and banners already strung out. The bleachers had just been repainted. It was looking as if this could be the best Rowdy Rodeo Days Extravaganza ever.

All of this was going down amazingly well — who would have believed it? Some of the early visitors had never, ever ridden a horse before. Dr. Mikey was in the stables, helping the ladies up into the saddles. Boy, is he ever good at that. Says he owes it to all the years of palming volleyballs at the rec center. The ladies seemed to like the assistance.

Charlie Mack was overseeing the setup in the south corral, where the Cheeseburger Barbecue Cook-Off Contest was to be held. This year we would have 19 contestants; most were annual repeat burger flippers.

Well, just when we all felt things were progressing in a smooth, orderly fashion, the weirdness began. Originally kept as a secret, and unbeknownst to everyone, was a mysterious entry for the Cheeseburger Cook-Off. A double announcement from Old Laffinatcha Meadows was revealed. The swanky twin brothers and direct descendants of King Letzal B. Laffinatcha — Imagona and Wergona — entered the contest and were accepted. A lot of people resented it, but Billy said they were qualified and would be welcomed, and that was final. The bright red–headed, bushy-haired duo had connected with Amy Jean Ruggles. Our girl spot welder had agreed to weld and join together two state-of-the-art Sears "Best of Class" Model 640B cookers.

The finished product was a thing of barbecue beauty. Nothing like this had ever been done before. The barbecues were slightly taller, which was perfect for the six-foot four-inch twins. The grill was ideally positioned for easily flippin' and scootin' those patties around. The physical units were enormous in that they were already individually used as commercial cookers, not like the typical puny backyard-and-patio Wcbers or Hamilton cookers. These Model 640B bad boys could barbecue for the masses.

Jesus could have used one of these hybrids when he was turning water into wine while dishing up loaves of unleavened bread, gefilte fish and tartar sauce to his followers somewhere near the Sea of Galilee. The area is now a members-only golf and tennis country club in the South Beach region of Israel.

Standing in front of these mega-cookers was a humbling experience. The dome-shaped lids were massive. The cookers were charcoal-colored over the tan base and trimmed in nickel plate, with solid jade lift handles. Inside each unit were two racks and two warming trays. They were set up for buns on one side and steamed veggies on the other. Each cooker was about five feet nine inches tall and 30 inches deep, and with the two joined together they were about seven feet across. They were designed with lots of storage space below and large polished-walnut food-cutting prep boards on each end. The heat-control dials were also trimmed with burnished walnut.

Being heavy, the double unit required a Skidoo-towing trailer's suspension with actual shocks, uprights and ball joints. The 10-inch magnesium spoke wheels were selected for the mounted radial-ply tires with all-weather tread design. They had chosen 175 x 10 x 40 Pirellis. A separate towing tongue could be fitted on either end for ease of maneuverability.

Imagona B. and Wergona B. Laffinatcha clearly wanted to win and had a take-no-prisoners attitude. In a humorous and lighthearted moment, they showed up for the dress rehearsal wearing cowboy hobo outfits. The twins looked like Emmett Kelly, a famous rodeo clown from many years ago.

The cheeseburger pros had been practising for months, perfecting both their technique and their timing. Also, to do it right, it takes research to find the freshest buns or special breads. Endless possibilities existed for getting the best cheeses or designer chef spreads. Of course, meat choices were also numerous. About half the contestants preferred to cook with lean hamburger meat only.

Anything else was sacrilege to them. The other contestants mixed a variety of meats, seasonings and exotic ingredients. The buns and other breads would be slathered with mayos and mustards and other popular accoutrements.

The Laffinatcha twins had the "doozy" of a cheeseburger recipe, as far as we were concerned. It even had Charlie Mack's undivided attention. That was a big deal given Charlie's history behind the charcoal. For the twins, it was two quarter-pound meat patties mushed together with minced yellow onion and mild jalapeños. The meat was 50:50 ground chuck steak and lean yearling pork. Hidden in between the patties were two medium slices of Lithuanian bratwurst with skin removed and two thin slices of sour pickle, sprinkled with finely chopped cilantro. Once the patties were joined and their edges sealed, they were ready to hit the preheated stainless steel chrome-plated grill.

First, it's five minutes a side, flip; then three, flip; then two, flip; then wait two more minutes for the world-class aged cheddar and Swiss to melt on top. Next, gently lift then slide the burger onto the San Francisco sourdough custom buns. After a big bite, the sour pickle hits you. Well, you gotta know that you're home-free from this point forward. Add some yucca dust and a case of Reindeer beer, and you will find yourself gobsmacked with all kinds of enlightenment and therefore truth and justice.

Charlie Mack was observed over at the Boogie Woogie Burger Bar having a very spirited conversation with the Laffinatcha twins for insurance reasons. They were drinking Reindeer beer. We were impressed that Maggie Anne had even heard of the Viking brew. Later on, as Charlie got up to leave, one of the twins slipped him a 100-dollar bill. Charlie tossed him a piece of paper, found out later to be the formula for infusing yucca dust into the burgers. He warned the twins to be conservative, as you could get too much "giddy-up" in your cheeseburger. Oh, what the heck, it was the Rowdy Rodeo Days Extravaganza, right here in Stickitville. It was party time. (Just ask Maynard.)

Billy checked the weather forecast for the next four days, and it looked great — warm and sunny. All of the events seemed to be well-organized. The only glitch so far was trying to have Luke the Drifter understand that getting the blindfolded turkey shoot on track meant that it was the shooters who were to be blindfolded, not the turkeys. Basically, he was ready to stand his ground and argue.

Perhaps he did have a point. One improvement this year was that all the turkeys would be in the same meadow, fenced in, and not being hunted all over town like last year.

Only after Joe Bob Pickens' shotgun had blown a large tom turkey off the First Baptist Church's steeple did common sense prevail. Since Joe Bob is nearly blind, he didn't have to be blindfolded. Some cried foul; others cried for the fowl.

Getting the parade started up was always stressful because somebody was bound to be out of sequence. This time seemed better; the main competing bands flipped a coin over who would lead and who would bring up the rear of the parade. The Stickitville kids lost and would bring up the rear. The Old Laffinatcha Sassy Rats Kids' Band thought they had it coming after the rude treatment received at the previous event.

The Color Guard went first, as always, then the bands followed behind the covered wagons, some being pulled by one horse; most had at least two, and a few had six horses. It was all very festive and the costumes were authentic. Kids gussied up their bicycles with ribbons and colorful crepe paper. They didn't know how to ride slowly, so some of them crashed into each other. All of a sudden, some of the parents got all bent out of shape, the fist fights started and a minor-size riot broke loose. Cow patties, rocks and bicycle parts sailed through the air.

"Steely-Eyed" Sheriff Geisler sent in the posse and broke up all the scuffles. The posse handed out yucca dust, and everybody regrouped; they were all hugs now, and so we marched on, towards the town square. It was noticed that Colonel JJ Eberhart's head was still missing from the rest of the statue. Billy said we were gonna get that fixed soon, someday, or maybe right away or possibly not ever.

The Old-Timers' Fiddle Float was being pulled by a spanking brand new John Deere 3500 tractor in the classic green and yellow colors. The 20 or so "Old Fiddle Farts," as they called themselves, could really only play one song. It was "The Orange Blossom Special" — they were awful at it. However, most people saw the humor and laughed a lot, whistling, clapping and having fun tossing flowers at them.

Natasha was mostly healed up after her "from-the-rafters plunge," just in time to be in the parade and to sit on top of Charlie Mack's new Dodge Ram tow truck. She sang the song "You Are My Sunshine" over and over and was backed up by the Scarlet Lesbionics Quartet. They sang it several times in four-part harmony. Those who knew her, which was virtually everyone, were teary-eyed.

Charlie wasn't happy about the large dent Natasha was putting in the rooftop of the new tow truck. Yep, a 250-plus-pound sugar babe will do it every time. At the end of the parade, she was lifted from the tow truck by its mechanical boom. The cable snapped and Natasha went *BOOM*, crashing to the asphalt. It was back to the hospital for her. Oh, by the way, the poor cat running across the street at the wrong time was squashed flat. Natasha had nailed it. The poor little black kitty was *"Adios, pussycat."*

The parade normally lasts about two hours, and the yucca dust was kicking in for many of our citizens as they worked their way over to the staging grounds near the rodeo arena. As with the Yucca Days Festival floats, the covered wagons were circled up into a pyramid shape and then set on fire — a truly amazing ritual, indeed. The parade horses were given the rest of the day off.

The Rowdy Rodeo Days Extravaganza officially began with the usual prayers for all of our citizens and with acknowledgments to the dignitaries.

There was the PM, the DM, the RM, the JM, the "Oh Him" and a pack of M&Ms. Both high school bands played one blaring, noisy non-tune, to the delight of our deaf community.

High up on Stickitville's mountainside, stashed in a bunker, was a rare vintage 50-millimeter Howitzer cannon. It was very loud when fired, and the blast would echo throughout the valley. The cannon was used to start civil functions such as our festivals and significant social adventures here in Stickitville.

So, for the first time ever, the hamlet of Old Laffinatcha Meadows — under the direction of King Letzal B. Laffinatcha's red-headed descendants, Princes Imagona B. and Wergona B. — decided it was time to get noticed. Lord knows how they located and purchased a WW II German Panzer tank. It was secretly driven at night up to a dugout and hidden under military artillery netting. The Panzer tank was now pointed right at Stickitville's edge. The 50-millimeter Howitzer was zeroed in at Old Laffinatcha Meadows. Hmmm!!

To signify the start of the rodeo, the Howitzer always fired five successive dummy rounds into the valley below. Of course, the projectiles had been removed from the shell casings. The reverberating sound of the Howitzer was deep and almost deafening. Birds squinted and ducked, squirrels fell from trees into a paws-up, comatose state, dogs and cats howled and meowed, and goats bleated, with some so upset they even missed a bleat. Cows and pigs were angry, non-hissing snakes wept openly, bumblebees bumbled and stumbled and were too afraid to sting anyone.

Old Laffinatcha Meadows was ready to show some Viking spunk. After many Reindeer beers and fistfuls of yucca dust, they opened fire with the Panzer tank's cannon. Well, the dumb bozos forgot to remove the business end of the shell casings, so the projectiles exploded, causing major damage to Stickitville's mountainside.

Billy and Captain Jim Carl called an emergency meeting. Mayor Spunky Dan was nowhere to be found, although someone said he was with Amy Jean over at the Back Room Meeting Place. They were shooting pool and watching old movies. An arrest warrant was issued for the princely twins Imagona and Wergona B. Laffinatcha. They would be charged with mayhem, noise violations and operating a vintage WW II tank without insurance or current licence plates.

Billy decided to give them a break and assessed a fine of not more than $138.70. They were also to provide one Reindeer beer to every ticket holder at the rodeo. Lithuanian-bratwurst-and-sour-pickle sandwiches were optional.

Jim Carl said that if they broke any more laws, he would personally have the twins' bright red bushy hair bleached and cut into a bowl-shape style like Moe's (of The Three Stooges fame). They were terrified at the prospect and promised to behave. Luke the Drifter said that the twins, as operators of both the Panzer and now the Howitzer military weapons, should be trained to fire cow patties into the sky at pilotless hot-air balloons. We think that Luke the Drifter has had far too many years of being overdosed on high-quality yucca dust.

The parade was over for another year and had been the best ever. The rival bands were friends now. The food booths were having a banner year, and the new outdoor car wash was very busy. The field hospital had worked mostly on people with frog bites.

The three-day Cheeseburger Barbecue Cook-Off Contest began in the evening with our Yucca Days Festival chicken and ribs champ, Mr. Charlie Mack Pearlman, as "Director in Charge." The Laffinatcha twins were focused and ready to make a name for Old Laffinatcha Meadows. Free samples of micro-mini-cheeseburgers were already circulating through the huge crowds. The next day would be sauce-blending day. Charlie Mack always used Geezer Mustard and Tabasco, but that was for chicken and ribs; he had always wondered how it might taste on a cheeseburger. Perhaps he would enter both cook-off contests next year.

At three o'clock, competition at the rodeo started. First up was calf roping, followed by bulldogging. This took up most of the afternoon. Cowboys from all over the world came to the Rowdy Rodeo Days Extravaganza to compete, eat cheeseburgers, smoke some yucca dust and chase our beautiful cowgirls. The really good cowboys could ride the wildest of our bucking broncos. Others, less fortunate, just got bucked off.

On the other hand, Darla May and Carla Jo said they occasionally liked the cheap thrill of getting gently bucked off. Amy Jean was seen going over to the Back Room Meeting Place with a couple of rough- and rowdy-looking cowpokes. We heard that she bucked them both off. With a silly big grin she smiled right through her knuckle-deep dimples, claiming that she was just "bucking around." Maggie Anne was asked if she'd ever been bucked off; she said not lately but could talk for hours about pro bonos and pro boners at the drive-in movie theater, and that's the buckin' truth.

The reigning bronc rider champ was a skinny Mexican lad named Sonny Barbados. When he smiled, his signature gold tooth flashed, pulsed and peeked through the handsome mustache that was smacked flat right there on his upper lip. All the older Girl Scouts whispered and giggled and thought he was one super-cute buckeroo.

The calf-roping and the bulldogging events had a few problems in that they had to use the same calf over and over for both. That was one beat-up and tired little heifer, no doubt. Natasha wanted to know why they didn't use actual bulldogs. She never got an answer, except that, for it to be fair, the cowboys would have to ride Shetland ponies. It just wouldn't have looked right but it darn sure would have looked funny, the rodeo clowns agreed. (Maynard rolled his eyes.)

The ladies' barrel races were scheduled for Saturday morning. The previous year's champion, and still beautiful, was Elva June Ridley. She could turn a horse on a dime and rocket to the next barrel, just a-twistin' and a-whippin' and a-spurrin' her way to another trophy. Nobody came even close to her finishing times. Or to her either, for that matter, until "El Capitán Pancho Sonny Villa" showed up. That wasn't his real name, of course. Sonny Barbados was often called that, however.

Well, as luck would have it, Elva June met our Mexican bronco rider right there at the Friday night Cheeseburger Barbecue Cook-Off Contest. She was smitten by Sonny's charm and good looks. He knew just how to flash that gold tooth of his, and they were an instant item. Sonny spoke in romantic Spanish phrases while serenading her on his Flamenco-style 12-string guitar.

After way too many Reindeer beers and fistful doses of yucca dust, Elva June led Sonny over to the barn where the horses were kept. She was very proud of her steed, a handsome horse named Fracas. He was a healthy three-year-old Tennessee Walker who was 16 hands high, with a beautiful and unusual sorrel color and a smooth coat. Fracas pawed the ground with his right hoof and gave Sonny a glaring and disapproving look. He could smell the booze, and he didn't like the gold tooth, either. (Maynard tipped his new Borsalino single-crease beaver felt cowboy hat.)

Our Mexican stud said to Elva June, "Let's go up and check out the loft. I'll play us some tunes, kiss your pretty face and show you how to do the Mexican-Amigo Sizzle-Style Hip-Shaking Bumpydance." He pulled out a pair of castanets, gave 'em a clickity-click-click-click and promised to show her the *cha-cha-chá* later on, "caballero-style."

She just wanted to get out of her skin-tight rodeo jeans and into something more comfortable. Sonny Barbados was there to help. Ya think? He strummed his 12-string guitar; Elva June strummed what he called his "Mucho Grande Burrito." The evening turned into a rompin,' stompin,' guacamole-snortin,' taco-snackin,' jalapeño-salsa-dippin' fiesta. Later they had a wonderful, heaven-sent chile relleno and fried chalupas topped with vanilla ice cream. Yummy Mexican pucky. Elva June Ridley was finally in love. (Really good stuff, Maynard.)

Morning came early for those who had partied just a bit too hard. There was much work to do before Saturday's activities got underway. Finding one's car keys seemed to be high on the to-do list. Captain Jim Carl told our "Steely-Eyed" Sheriff to start bustin' heads and to get this Rowdy Rodeo show up and running before noon. Animals needed to be fed, watered and groomed, and barn stalls cleaned and stocked. Fans would be pouring into the arena soon. Security was at an all-time high due to the "Canyon Cannon Duel." The Howitzer and the Panzer tank had been hauled off by Pearlman Towing to Natasha's Salvage Yard.

It was decided that the kickoff to the day's festivities would be started by a chubby Cub Scout playing "A Call to Arms" on a bugle instead of a harmonica. Elva June Ridley thought he should play "Blame It on the Bossa Nova or the Macarena." Her head was pounding.

* * *

You, my esteemed readers, are due to get an update on Stinky, and also on officers Slats O'Reilly and Snapper McCoy. It's difficult to work them in now, as this saga has taken on a life of its own with the Rowdy Rodeo Days Extravaganza jumping somewhat ahead of our story. Thus I find it necessary to rewind a bit and get some balance to this brain drain I'm experiencing.

Back at the scene of the police van that crashed in the Crow Valley, Stinky had gotten off easy with just a headache and a sprained finger. Officers Slats and Snapper, while left dangling from their seat belts in the back of the van, suffered minor bruises and the embarrassment of having been kidnapped by Stinky. Our Hero Billy grilled Stinky for his side of the story but said he would be fair if Stinky came clean and told the truth. Stinky wanted the assurance that Slats and Snapper would also have to own up with their side of this sordid tale.

Long story short, Stinky was running drugs and operating a cash-laundering service for the Carmen Miranda Caramba Cartel out of Central Mexico via Juarez and the mighty Rio Grande. His Mexican connections were impeccable, as they were high up in the political structures of civic power, all controlled by Juan Pablo Mateus and his buddy Luca Don Genero. This meant that he was not in any trouble at all. He knew it, Our Hero Billy knew it, Jim Carl knew it, and Luke the Drifter knew it. All of this could be linked to the Roby E. Smith Memorial Institute. Dark and deep in our history are the smoldering ruins of a lost and nearly long-forgotten story.

* * *

This is the tale of Arthur Ray Rahn, a.k.a. Luke the Drifter, and a historical event involving Jim Carl Lillard. Luke and Jim Carl knew long ago that this story would have to surface eventually. The adventure began with a company gathering somewhere in West Virginia. Something to do with the clothing industry and a sales meeting of sorts. Jim was in a day early for orientation and to get a leg up on the bar girls at their hotel. Well, good ol' Mr. Lillard got himself blasted with tequila shooters, weed and possibly a bar of soap. Who knew? The commotion began in his room when he decided that the right thing to do was to start howling like a wolf tripping out on a full-moonlight night filled with sparkling moonbeam dust. Throw in a little mescaline, and you have got yourself a first-class out-of-body experience right there in the Riverside Motel somewhere in West Virginia. Somehow, the next day, Jim made it to the meeting and power-suffered through a major hangover. It was nearly noon before he could say much more than "Huh," and "Uh-huh." (Maynard was appalled but understood.)

Later in the day, the rest of the sales force started showing up. The management and staff had thought it would be novel, if not hilarious, to have Arthur Ray Rahn be Jim Carl's roommate for the sales meeting. Both of these men were about six foot six inches tall — Jim from Texas, Arthur from Louisiana. Upon checking in, Arthur heard the story of Jim's howling until the wee hours, which of course kept everyone in the hotel awake all night. Art knew right from the start that he had the right roommate even before he met him. He made his way to the room, walked in and said, "Hi, you must be the Wolfman." Jim stood up and, with an eyeball-to-eyeball connection, looked straight back at Art and countered, "Yep, and you must be Luke the Drifter." The names stuck. This meeting started a long-term friendship that was a natural for a pair of garden-variety drug abusers.

Years later, Jim Carl moved on to a great job opportunity in Dallas, Texas, with big bucks and big responsibility. Yours Truly had a small hand in helping him land this plum of a job. To celebrate this event, Jim and his wife, Jan, took me and my wife, Gayle, out to a plushy, expensive restaurant for dinner. It was a long evening, and we all got pretty hammered. In fact, it was a "knee-walking, commode-hugging" stumble over to the parking lot to go home. Assuming we could find home. So it was up and over to the North Dallas Tollway. Jim always liked to drive fast, and this night was no exception. It was about midnight or later and we had Jan's Mustang up to 80 or 90 mph, when the red lights of the tollway cop cruiser started blinking and flashing and the sirens were blaring their best high-decibel, ear-damaging song.

The cops both looked to be about 19 years old and had shaved at least once. However, their shoes were shined and their collar brass was polished and spotless. They politely asked us all to get out of the Mustang and to stand over on the edge of the tollway. Cars were zooming by us at arm's length while the rookie cops searched the car. Jim Carl had just stuck a full ounce of Acapulco Gold over the visor; the cops never saw it. After the search, the tough-guy cop said, "OK, how much have you all had to drink?" I started to give them a person-by-person, drink-by-drink rundown and was told to "shut the fook up." The cop said to Jim — who, as previously mentioned, is six foot six — "Okay Shorty," with a cocky smile and a smirk, "let's have the story, and by the way, I want everyone's driver's licence, home address and phone number."

Jim launched into his explanation, which was the best get-out-of-jail story I'd ever heard: "Well, Officer, I have just returned from Vietnam on leave and am trying to get back with my wife, as we have recently separated. I'm only here for another three days, then it's back to Saigon and the war. Sorry, I don't have my licence — somehow it got lost on the trip back home."

The tough-guy cop, not being fazed or moved by Big Jim's story, said, "Okay, what's your name?"

Jim sort of swallowed, took an enormous deep breath and said, straight-faced, "Sir, my name is Roby E. Smith." Stunned, I damn near fell down. I was sure we were all headed to jail. Jan, Jim's wife, was frozen in time. Gayle broke out laughing.

At this very strange moment, another car, a Porsche, roared by all of us going at least 100 mph. The cops decided to chase the car down, so they handed Jim his keys, told us to "wait right here" and just left us there on the tollway. Jan looked at Jim and said, "Mind if I drive, Shorty?"

Roby became an icon to all our friends, and the story became legend. By the way, Roby is pronounced "Row-bee" not "Rob-ee." The Roby E. Smith Memorial Institute became respected, and to this day it benefits lost souls — and gets huge government funding, to boot. So, over 40 years later, our Jim Carl Lillard is still called Roby by many of his friends.

* * *

Back to our rodeo in Stickitville. No one had predicted it, but a ferocious thunderstorm blew in and soaked everything. Light rain continued and the claps of thunder frightened all the animals; many simply refused to participate. The broncos wouldn't buck, the one calf wouldn't allow itself to be roped or bulldogged, and the Brahma bulls just took the day off and cruised the arena at will. At least they were friendly. Billy said he'd never seen anything like it before. Joe Bob suggested getting out the electric cattle prods and moving the animals back in line. By golly, they had a job to do, right? "You betchum, Red Ryder," said Little Beaver.

Elva June Ridley's horse slipped and went *ka-skwoosh* in the mud on the second turn during a practice run. Elva June was okay, but we thought Fracas might have to be put down. Well, right at the last moment, who should show up but Officer Snapper McCoy on the Cushman. He downshifted the scooter to a screeching halt.

The fear — and the sheer terror — caused by McCoy's presence sparked new life into Elva June's horse, and Fracas ran the barrels by himself four times, breaking all the riderless barrel race records. The barn pigeons took a victory lap for him, and Fritz proudly perched himself on the saddle horn, tucked the reins under his wing and rode

Mr. Fracas back to his stall. One heck of a brave parrot. With precision wing flapping, the pigeons flew towards the town square, right over Colonel JJ Eberhart's still headless statue. This ceremonial in-flight pigeon dump in military formation was designed exclusively for our heroes, leaders and other rock stars, including Fracas.

Well, due to the inclement weather (And don't you feel good about the word *inclement*? Reading and saying the word makes one feel intellectual, powerful and smug. It ranks right up there with *mayonnaise*, *linoleum* and *germane*.), most people at the rodeo found other things to do. They ate some really good food from our excellent booths selling hot dogs, burgers and even a few bratwurst-and-sour-pickle sandwiches. Kids hated the sandwiches; Fritz loved them, and summarily cursed the kids — in German, of course.

Sonny Barbados was nowhere to be found, and since he was the champ bronc rider, we were forced to consider replacing him in the lineup with Dr. Mikey Lamar Cook. Mikey packed himself up with yucca dust and "brave pills" and said he would do it, but bronc horses only — no calf ropin,' no bulldoggin' and certainly no Brahma bull ridin.'

Elva June Ridley was heartbroken upon realizing that she had been dumped by the charming Mexican bandito. She thought of his shiny gold tooth, and the clickity-click-click-and-clack rhythms from his castanets, not to mention the memory of the evening in the loft, the 12-string guitar strumming and the consuming of a dusty magic burrito, all of it. *Cha-cha-chá.*

Mayor Spunky Dan Carlson was notified that Sonny Barbados had been seen whippin' and spurrin' his 1978 Ford Bronco towards Old Laffinatcha Meadows and the caves further up the valley. Seems he hadn't informed Consuelo Rodriguez, his gorgeous and wealthy Mexican girlfriend, about the Rowdy Rodeo Days Extravaganza here in Stickitville. Somehow Consuelo had gotten wind of his evening and his romantic "in the loft" sayings and 12-string guitar strumming with Elva June Ridley. Consuelo had her very sharp-edged switchblade knife with the ebony handle tucked into her Coyote Sportswear five-pocket jeans. Her plan was simple: find Sonny Barbados and explain to him that she wasn't going to share the dusty magic burrito with some saddle horn–grabbing, barrel-racing Rodeo Queen. Frankly, she was prepared to slowly slice off his *huevos* and put them in a pickle jar. He believed she would do it, so it was the final "big vamoose and over the hill" for Sonny.

Well, you might have guessed that Consuelo would run into none other than Joe Bob Pickens eventually. Oh my, oh boy, here we go. It happened at the Boogie Woogie Burger Bar — where else? Joe Bob had heard via the *Trashy Pipeline Gazette* news source that a very lovely *señorita* had been jilted by her Mexican champ bronc rider. It was in an "eye-twitch blink" that our nearly blind local caught enough of a glimpse to tractor-beam up and down the bar with "hot babe"-searching, laser-tracking qualities. Soon he discovered this Mexican beauty, who immediately grabbed his absolute attention. Rarely did Joe Bob take out his secret eyeglasses and secretly clean them. He had to be certain; after all, he's nearly blind, you know. Uh-huh.

For sure, Joe Bob had had his share of wonderful and lovely ladies, and not just because of the reputation borne by his legendary charm and style. He was basically a fine, good-looking man, well-groomed and well-spoken. After realizing that Consuelo was perfect and that she could not be any more stunning, Joe Bob had a revelation. Suddenly he did the unbelievable. He called Our Hero Billy and said he wanted to introduce him to a very nice and beautiful Mexican lass. Joe Bob said he had a feeling she might be the right one for him.

He was correct. To celebrate, Maggie Anne put a case of Carta Blanca beer on ice, dimmed the lights and put on slow-dancing music. The Cardoza Playboys and everyone else went, "Oooh," and "Ahhh," with a great, big Rowdy Rodeo Days Extravaganza sigh and smile.

The rain and wind had slowed the pace on Saturday, but our citizens were hardy and tough and could take a lot. The Brahma bull riders decided to wait till Sunday and do a double show. Not sure how the bulls felt about it, but they are usually grumpy anyway. To give rodeo fans their money's worth, Billy and Grand Marshal Pearlman decided to rerun all the events, including the bands and the parade, as long as there was daylight and they all agreed.

Sonny Barbados was the only dropout, because he was hiding from Consuelo. He didn't need to, as Consuelo and Billy had fallen in love — in record time, I might add. Maybe they deserved to get a prize for it. Joe Bob just clicked his teeth and cut his conquest losses. He had plenty of trophies, probably more than most.

Elva June was ready to ride the barrels again, and Dr. Mikey checked out all the bucking bronco horses. The calf ropin' and bulldoggin' was back on track. Sheriff Eddie Wayne signed up to ride the Brahma bulls; said he needed the money. Probably for his new boat.

If Sunday went as well as planned, the Rowdy Rodeo Days Extravaganza would be deemed a huge success. We were only missing 11 hot-air balloons so far. Not bad, considering that 75 had left in a mass ascension at the launching area in the early morning. We expected to get most of them back. There was a little concern over the 14 children in the kiddie group who were still missing. However, the search-and-rescue guys were all at the Boogie Woogie Burger Bar and ready to spring into action if need be. The Saturday night parties and the north side arena barn dance were all set up right across from Natasha's Salvage Yard.

The Cheeseburger Contest winners would be announced at 6 p.m. The red-headed Laffinatcha twins were the favorites to win, which would bring in a first-time trophy for that community. Imagona B. and Wergona B. promised that if they won, they would dance the Jingo-Jango Viking Jig, which includes tossing sheep over a 12-foot-high bonfire.

The winner would get a case of Reindeer beer and a month's supply of yucca dust.

The cowboy bands were really good and offered lessons on how to dance the Virginia Reel, the Western Two-Step, the Cowboy Waltz, the Cotton-Eyed Joe and the Schottische. Line dancing was always a big hit with the younger crowd. There was also a new star from Lubbock, Texas — a real cowgirl singer named Olivia Newton Polly Parton. She sang "sad old lonesome" cattle-drive songs. The seniors loved her and hollered for more.

The Sunday rodeo events went off on schedule. The parade was also well attended by thousands of gawkers and onlookers. The Stickitville Kids' Band and the Sassy Rats Kids' Band switched ends just for added interest. They even switched non-tunes, including "Onward Roswell." They would have switched their brand new band uniforms, but that would have been too complicated.

Charlie Mack temporarily left his duties as Grand Marshal to lead the festivities as Drum Major. The crowd went wild. The man was clearly the very best. The bands marched several laps around the arena, before the bronc riding took front and center. There was much buzzing and whispering about why the world champ bronc rider wasn't there. It was a lover's quarrel and "kaffuffel," and Sonny Barbados had lost out to Our Hero Billy. Some said that his gold tooth had clearly pulsed, flickered and dimmed. Billy and Consuelo were still at the Boogie Woogie Burger Bar; Maggie Anne had left them the keys to the bar and told them to stay as long they liked, then please lock the place up. They were in love. Ahhh!!!

To add to the bronc-riding trophy, Dr. Mikey Cook announced that if your parking stall number ended in zero, you could claim a free medical exam at the rodeo clinic. The cowboy guys murmured but didn't say much. The cowgirls, on the other hand, were all chatty about it. What really surprised everyone was that Dr. Mikey rode all three horses to the bell and won the championship bronc rider's trophy. He received a cash prize of $13,274.

Next up was the calf-roping and bulldogging competition. The PRO found two more healthy calves, plus the original one. This enhanced the event by quite a lot. They also took Natasha's comments about using real bulldogs to heart, and somebody showed up with two full-blooded overweight English bulldogs. Natasha watched it on TV from the hospital and was pleased with herself. The calves were offended by these immigrant "hoity-toity dogs" with their strange British barking accents. "A spot of tea with crumpets." "My fanny!! I say, how 'bout some rattlesnake meat and a dozen whiskey shooters?" Those prissy dogs weren't cowboy enough at all — no siree bobtail. The locals would seek a petition to ban them from next year's Rowdy Rodeo Days Extravaganza. More victory laps were taken, with colorful flags and the bands blaring more non-tune songs; the barn pigeons were all in sync, ready for military formation if necessary.

The big event of the rodeo was always the Brahma bull rider competition. This year Our Hero Billy, Captain Jim Carl, Sheriff Eddie Wayne, Luke the Drifter, Stinky and the entire bunch of Cardoza Playboys signed in and suited up for the bull ride. Somebody was surely going to die. Officers Slats O'Reilly and Snapper McCoy mysteriously sneaked off to the Stickitville Fish Hatchery, no doubt for more Shark Games and rooftop star gazing.

Charlie Mack led the bands to a final, almost ear-blasting glory. Spunky Dan Carlson was up in the announcer's booth. Joe Bob clicked his teeth and started looking for Darla May and Carla Jo. He also put in a call for Amy Jean over at the Back Room Meeting Place. He could be such a greedy man, and sometimes quite conceited. The 25 pom-pom cheerleaders and majorettes were all spoken for. The Six Lovely Fancy Line Dancers were unavailable due to work contracts. Maggie Anne was busy making beef and gerbil tacos at the Boogie Woogie Burger Bar. Our beautiful Consuelo was in the gilded golden lounge of her own romantic thoughts and fantasies. She was planning a new adventure with Billy. They were in love — ahhhh!! Even the red-headed Laffinatcha twins were moved to tears.

That was it!! The Rowdy Rodeo Days Extravaganza was done. The cowboy sunset had a special orange glow and vibe to it that evening. The throngs of spectators were quiet but satisfied as they shuffled back to their own realities. Some people were looking frantically for their parking stall numbers and searching for the lucky number zero. The cheap crowd, no doubt. There was the final clink of champagne in a beer bottle, and a last burger. The memories — ah, the memories.

Epilogue

Hold on!! "Stop the presses," as they would say in *Superman 2* — have we forgotten something here, folks? "You betchum, Red Ryder," said Little Beaver. He would know, of course.

Along with the dignitaries in the announcer's booth were Fritz Von Schwanstooker the parrot and Freddie the leprechaun. Aha, so how many of you noticed that they've been missing lately from this far-fetched and silly mountain drama?

Fritz and Freddie have fooled everyone, and no one's noticed. It's the most shocking and outrageous scam of scams here in the history of Stickitville and Old Laffinatcha Meadows. I predict it will go down in *Book of the Ages* for all to see and read.

* * *

Okay, folks — big finish now. Fritz and Freddie are both wearing their motorcycle gang vests. Fritz pulls on his WW II fighter pilot's cap and his red scarf. Freddie (in his traditional leprechaun suit) hops up on Fritz's left wing shoulder. As mentioned before, I don't know why; it's just the way it is. Left side only, please. I guess Freddie will have to nuzzle and chew on the flap of the aviator cap.

Fritz launches the two of them into full-wing soaring mode. Freddie is loving it. Just then, Fritz spots officers Slats O'Reilly and Snapper McCoy racing up the mountain road on Snapper's 1948 red Cushman Road King two-speed side-shifter scooter, obviously headed towards the Stickitville Fish Hatchery. They all wave, whoop and holler at each other. Snapper hits a pothole and darn near crashes the scooter. With that, Fritz and Freddie zoom on up the valley towards the cave where the Howitzer and the WW II Panzer tank have been secretly moved to.

Once inside the cave, Freddie lights a candle and they both push a fairly large boulder aside, opening up a chamber where, on an old wooden table similar to one you might find at Geppetto and Hans's Trusty Taxidermy Shop, there is a dark brown leather pouch with a shoulder strap. It is about the size of Wonder Woman's large clutch recently purchased at Gucci. In the pouch are the bank receipts of deposits totaling three to four million dollars. It seems that what was in those brown butcher paper–wrapped packages had an enormous value. Ya think? Not to mention the one million fresh Yankee bucks that were in the five full-size all-leather matching suitcases.

The candle is then blown out, and our parrot, Fritz Von Schwanstooker, and Freddie, the leprechaun-looking fellow, take off for parts unknown. The flight takes them over puffy clouds, through a rainbow and into the sunset. The thermals lift them into the quietness of space.

Freddie, with a smug look on his face, looks at Fritz the parrot and says, "OK, dude, I know you're a fraud, Fritz, so what's with the phony German accent? Hmmm? I happen to know that you are a Purple Robe Harvard lawyer and a world-class traveler. I'm aware that you speak at least five languages fluently. Might I ask, what is your real name, and what is your quest in life?"

Without hesitation the parrot answers, "My name is Gerald Dwight McBride. My friend is Little Dickie Wyly. We seek enlightenment and therefore truth and justice. That is our quest."

Gray shades of silence hover, then fading upward into the clouds above they hear: "Onward Roswell… Onward Roswell… Ta-dah, ta-dah, ta-da-da-da."

Gerald Dwight McBride shrugs, then folds his wings neatly to his shoulders to acknowledge Freddie. All of a sudden, without warning, Freddie says, "Quick, chew this 'Foof-Poof Gum' — it will make you invisible. I can see the glint of shotgun barrels down at the Stickitville Country Club and Golf Course, right beside the Dead Ducks Pond and behind the hunter's shooting blind."

The airspace crackles, booms and sputters as shots ring out against the buttermilk skies. *BAM BAM BAM* and another *BAM*. If Foof-Poof works as it's supposed to, they'll be lucky; and if not, it'll be *Pfffphssittt* — therefore curtains for both of them.

*   *   *

Watch for the definite possibility of a sequel. You might be wondering where the rest of the money went. (Just ask Maynard; he's in charge of the good stuff.)

Acknowledgments

I would like to thank the many personal friends who encouraged me and the professional people who worked tirelessly to bring this book to completion and out there for you to endure and enjoy. First, Anne Ryall, who did the copy editing, among other major duties. Next, Larry Shwedyk, who created the incredible artwork on the front cover. Then Tiffany Meyer, who was a genius at combining the various elements so that the illustration expresses the spirit of this Saga. Colleen Campbell gave valuable feedback and artfully created the landscape background for the cover. A big thank you to my wonderfully crazy friends — Billy Cardoza, Terry Wilmot, Jim Lillard, Eddie Geisler, Charles Pearlman, Clint Cawsey and Bob Snape — who supported me and provided inspiration for the book. Maynard set the standard and supplied constant leadership (he is, of course, the itinerant man of knowledge).

About the Author

Richard Wyly has enjoyed entertaining others ever since he was about two years old, when he began belting out classic American folk songs while taking center stage on the family coffee table. He grew up in Roswell, New Mexico, spending much of his childhood on the farms and ranches of relatives. His extensive background in the apparel industry dates back to when he began working for his parents in their children's clothing business at age 10. He went on to become the co-owner, with his brother, Victor, of a menswear store and ski shop and later a sales rep for clothing manufacturers in California and other Western states. Richard fondly remembers when Saturday matinées cost a quarter, and he has been a lifelong fan of old Western movies and their stars. A former vintage car racer, motorcycle enthusiast and marathon runner, he currently lives in Canmore, Alberta, in the Canadian Rockies. Watch for future *Tales of Wonder* titles.

CPSIA information can be obtained
at www.ICGtesting.com
Printed in the USA
LVHW081145110420
652880LV00002B/5